By J. Kenner

THE STARK TRILOGY
  Release Me
  Claim Me
  Complete Me

STARK EVER AFTER NOVELLAS
  Take Me
  Have Me
  Play My Game
  Seduce Me
  Unwrap Me
  Deepest Kiss

STARK INTERNATIONAL NOVELS
  THE JACKSON STEELE TRILOGY
  Say My Name
  On My Knees
  Under My Skin
  THE DIRTIEST TRILOGY
  Dirtiest Secret
  Hottest Mess
  Sweetest Taboo

MOST WANTED SERIES
  Wanted
  Heated
  Ignited

sweetest taboo

sweetest

taboo

A STARK INTERNATIONAL NOVEL

J. KENNER

 Bantam Books New York

Published in the United States by Bantam, an imprint of Random House, a division of Penguin Random House LLC, New York.

BANTAM BOOKS and the HOUSE colophon are registered trademarks of Penguin Random House LLC.

Library of Congress Cataloging-in-Publication Data
Names: Kenner, Julie, author.
Title: Sweetest taboo / J. Kenner.
Description: New York : Bantam, 2016. | Series: S.I.N. (Stark International Novel) ; 6
Identifiers: LCCN 2016027540 (print) |
LCCN 2016034337 (ebook) | ISBN 9781101967492 (softcover) |
ISBN 9781101967508 (ebook)
Subjects: LCSH: Man-woman relationships—Fiction. |
Billionaires—Fiction. | BISAC: FICTION / Romance / Contemporary. | FICTION / Contemporary Women. |
FICTION / Romance / Suspense. | GSAFD: Romantic suspense fiction. | Erotic fiction.
Classification: LCC PS3611.E665 S94 2016 (print) |
LCC PS3611.E665 (ebook) | DDC 813/.6—dc23
LC record available at https://lccn.loc.gov/2016027540

Printed in the United States of America on acid-free paper

randomhousebooks.com

9 8 7 6 5 4 3 2 1

sweetest taboo

She'd thought Dallas would be hers by now.

She'd thought he would understand that it was inevitable.

Was it her fault that she had to hurry him along? That she had to make him see?

Where love was concerned, a girl had to do what she had to do, and Dallas Sykes was a man with a flair for the dramatic. He liked a show. He liked to make a statement.

He might be angry at first; she understood that. Because her plan to clear the path to him was—what? Radical? Dangerous?

No. Imperative. She had no choice, really. He was, quite simply, hers. The world just didn't realize that yet.

More importantly, Dallas didn't realize that yet.

She didn't understand how he could not know. Between them it had been special. It had been pure. Not like those sluts he'd drawn into his bed. Not like this ridiculous affair with his sister, all the more vile because it was splashed all over social media, their shame making headlines and turning stomachs.

She'd never considered him dim-witted, but maybe he was.

Because he should know. He should understand. And yet he didn't.

But that was okay. He would soon enough.

And then . . .

Well, and then he'd truly be hers.

Again.

1

Gone Girl

"She's not here. Goddammit, she's not here."

Dallas Sykes's blood burned with dread and fear curled in his gut like acid as he stalked down the dark, residential block of Eighty-Second Street, his eyes scanning every nook and cranny, searching for a woman he knew wasn't there.

This late, the street was deserted, the residents tucked safe in their beds behind the darkened windows of the Upper West Side townhouses that rose like the wall of an inescapable maze on either side of Dallas.

Where? Where the fuck was she?

The area was too damn dark, the few door lights far too dim to be any help at all. Instead, Dallas used the light on his phone to cut through the night as he scoured every damn inch of the street for some sign of Jane. A broken fingernail. A shoe.

God forbid, even blood.

He shuddered, trying to push back his terror. He wasn't succeeding.

This was his fault, goddammit. *His.*

He'd hidden the truth from Jane, thinking he was making it better. That he was sparing her more pain. But those buried secrets had burst free, wild and vicious and dangerous. And now she was gone. Missing. Possibly dead—except she couldn't be dead; the thought was too big, too horrible to even wrap his mind around.

But captive? Oh, dear Christ, what if she'd been thrust back into the horror of their childhood, and all because of him?

"Keep looking." Liam's voice—firm, controlled—filtered through the speaker. "I'm showing a signal."

"Of course I'm going to keep looking," Dallas snapped. "But she's not here." His voice rose, matching his escalating fear. "And neither is her damn phone."

"Stay with me, Dallas. You can't help her if you lose your shit."

"*Fuck*." A fresh wave of fear crested inside him, and Dallas had to tighten his grip on his own phone in order to fight the almost irresistible urge to hurl the damn thing to the ground. But he couldn't. As impotent as his smart phone was at the moment, it was his lifeline to her.

Jane.

His heart. His soul.

The one person in all the world he craved, needed, *loved* more than any other.

And Liam was right—he couldn't help her if he lost control. If he let himself drown in fear and memories.

So he wouldn't. He'd stay on the street. He'd search. He'd follow every lead. But in the end, he would find her because no other option was even conceivable. He'd find her, he'd rescue her, and then he'd kill the fucking bitch who'd taken her.

Fighting a shudder, he once again looked at the image that someone had sent to him from her phone.

Jane. Beaten and battered.

Jane. Unconscious and helpless on a sidewalk. *This* sidewalk. Or at least somewhere near here, because Liam was tracking her phone to these coordinates. So where the hell was she?

Slowly, he drew in a breath, then exhaled with just as much precision. "You're sure this is the location?"

"I'm sure. I'm logged in to her account. I can see the phone's location on the map. And we're looking at a circumference of about eight meters."

Dallas nodded, trusting his friend because he knew damn well that he couldn't rely on himself. He wasn't thinking straight at all. The last thing he remembered with any clarity was standing in the new apartment that he shared with Jane, a little shell-shocked after she'd laid into him about the secrets he'd been keeping. She'd stormed out, and he'd forced himself to hold back, knowing that she needed to get her anger out of her system. He'd expected her to take a walk, maybe visit her friend Brody.

He hadn't expected that she would be attacked. Taken.

He hadn't expected a repeat of their goddamn childhood.

And he sure as hell hadn't anticipated that his phone would ping with a text message showing Jane splayed out on the street, her eyes closed and her face battered.

That image had been horrible enough. But what really gave him chills was the carnival-style mask on the ground next to her prone form. A mask just like the one the Woman had worn when she'd entered their cell all those years ago. Like she'd worn when she took him away from Jane. When she'd tortured him for hours—*days*—on end.

His stomach twisted as his mind filled with images of what she'd done to him. Only this time, it wasn't Dallas who was the victim of the Woman's cruel abuse, but Jane.

No. Please, God, no.

"No mask, no Jane. Christ, Liam, where the fuck is she?"

"The guys are on their way. They'll start going door to door. We'll find her," Liam said, but Dallas could hear the fear in his voice, too.

He turned in a circle as he examined the empty street in this quiet, residential area. Jane had to be somewhere, and maybe the Woman had dragged her into one of these brownstones. Maybe someone had seen something, heard something. But the street was empty now. Noah and Tony would go door to door looking for witnesses. But that would take time.

Time Jane might not have.

Her attacker could have taken her anywhere. But she could also be right there, just meters away. She could be watching from a window, her hands tied, her mouth gagged, hope fading as she saw him fumbling in the dark.

Fuck that.

Dallas took another hard look at the area he'd already scoured. No phone.

He stepped off the sidewalk and into the street. Same as it had been two minutes ago. Except . . .

"The gutter," he said to Liam even as he dropped to his hands and knees, then thrust his arm in up to the shoulder. Absurd, really. If the phone was down there, it would be well out of reach in the storm drain, ready to be washed away with the next rain. He couldn't get to it, not without—

"I have it." Then he spit out a curse. Because so the fuck what? The phone wasn't the woman, and he still didn't have Jane. And now he knew with absolute certainty that she wasn't with her phone.

Fuck.

"Open her photos," Liam ordered. "There wasn't any location information buried in the picture you received or the text. Maybe the photo was taken in another block. Maybe they attacked her somewhere else and ditched the phone here."

"Already on it," Dallas said, a spring of hope bubbling as he tapped and swiped the screen to get the photo to open. Sure enough, there was location information attached. He read the GPS coordinates off to Liam, his body tense as he waited for Liam to send him to a new location.

But all Liam did was whisper a soft "*Goddammit.*"

Dallas didn't need to hear more. He knew what that meant. His last line to Jane had been severed.

He cocked his head, thinking.

Maybe not the last, after all.

"Colin awake?"

"Coming around," Liam said. "We loaded him up with a shit-ton of tranqs, but they're starting to wear off. I was about to dose him again. Keep him under until Quince can get here from London."

"No," Dallas said. "Let him wake up. I'm coming in."

2

In the Box

Dallas had known Colin West since he was five years old. He'd grown up around the man. He'd comforted Jane when Colin's boneheaded decisions had put her in danger. He'd held her when Lisa, their mom, had filed suit to terminate Colin's parental rights so that Eli—Dallas's uncle and adoptive father—could adopt Jane, making Dallas and Jane full-blown brother and sister.

Dallas never had doubts that Colin could be a dickwad. After all, the guy had served jail time for insider trading, then followed that with a second stint for tax fraud. He'd made bad decisions and he'd run with the wrong crowd.

But Dallas had also seen the way Colin had comforted Jane after the kidnapping. When she was vulnerable and confused and needed to get away from her family. What had hurt the most was that it was Dallas she'd been trying to escape. Their connection—their passion—had sustained them in captivity. But it had been the one thing they absolutely could not take with them beyond those concrete walls.

So she'd left. Closed herself off. And turned to Colin for support.

Dallas had hated the distance, but he'd been grateful for Colin, who had seemingly put aside his hurt at having his rights terminated in order to be there for his daughter. So grateful, in fact, that Dallas and Colin had forged their own friendship as Dallas had moved into adulthood. And over time, Colin and his new wife, Adele, had become part of Dallas's circle of friends.

Never once had Dallas suspected that Colin might have been the force behind the kidnapping of Jane and Dallas. Never once had it even crossed his mind that the man he'd grown up around—the man who Jane still loved like a father—had been the Jailer. The man who'd locked them in a room. The man who'd whispered to Dallas that he deserved every bit of agony he suffered in captivity.

The man who allowed the Woman to play her sadistic, sexual games on a fifteen-year-old boy.

Now he suspected it. Hell, now he believed it.

It made him sick, but he believed it.

And as he sped down the near-empty street on the classic Ducati Darmah he'd bought in college, all he could think was that he had to get to Colin. He had to find Jane. Because at the end of the day, she was the only one who mattered. And once he stepped into the room with that son of a bitch, there was no way Colin was getting out alive until Dallas had answers.

He made a hard right, then opened the bike up when he saw that the lane was clear. He was going too damn fast, and he knew it, but he couldn't slow down. Not when memories of Colin still filled his head. Not when he was trying to escape the lingering memory of Jane's face when she'd told him to go.

And certainly not when the Jailer's voice still whispered in his ear, as fresh and hard as it had been almost eighteen years ago.

Do you think he's going to come for you, that man you call your father? Do you think he loves you enough to pay the price to keep you?

You better hope so.

You better hope you're more to him than just another fucking showpiece to set on his mantel. One more acquisition in the great Eli Sykes's collection.

I'll tell you a secret—I hope so, too. Because you aren't worth the air you breathe. And if he doesn't pay to get you back, I don't know why the hell I should bother to keep you alive.

With a violent jerk to the handlebars, Dallas skidded to a stop two blocks from his destination, his breath coming hard. He sat a moment, looking down the street at a half-demolished East Harlem grocery store as he tried to push the memories back. Tried to get his shit together.

He wasn't that scared teenager anymore. He was a grown man, and a powerful one at that. And he intended to wield a little of that power right now.

It was time to shove aside his goddamn memories.

It was time to get Jane back. Over an hour had passed since that horrible text had arrived in his inbox, and every second was like a knife in his gut. She needed him to be focused. Smart.

She needed him to find her, to protect her the way he'd always promised he would. And he damn sure wasn't going to let her down.

Determined, he slid off the bike and then walked toward the building that Deliverance had purchased eighteen months ago, the ownership hidden behind an impenetrable wall of shell corporations and fake foreign investors.

As far as the public was concerned, the run-down market in the transitional neighborhood was being demolished and converted into a luxury residential project. And technically, that was true. It just happened that the conversion was going at a snail's pace. And in the meantime, the project was perfect camouflage for the entrance to Deliverance's Manhattan operations center.

Dallas had formed Deliverance with the hope of locating his and Jane's kidnappers—their *past* kidnappers. Now five men—Dallas, Liam, Quince, Tony, and Noah—made up the ultra-secret, elite vigilante team that did whatever it took to locate and rescue kidnap victims. But never once had Dallas anticipated that he would use Deliverance's resources to search for Jane, and the irony of that reality sat heavy in his gut.

Ironic or not, Dallas was grateful that Deliverance existed. It may have been his brainchild, but Dallas was only a small part of the reason the organization was so damned effective. He'd populated it with men he knew and trusted. And, more importantly, who were exceptionally good at their jobs. Right now, Liam was running the operation from inside the center. Noah and Tony were armed with fake police badges and going door to door on the Upper West Side street where Dallas had found Jane's phone. And Quince—who was also an MI6 agent—was on his way back from London.

On any other mission, Dallas would want Quince in the interrogation room. The man had acquired a unique skill set, after all. But this time, Dallas was grateful his friend was away. Because all Dallas wanted at the moment was to curl his fingers around Colin's throat until the fucker confessed to everything. Until he revealed who the Woman was and where she'd taken Jane.

Dallas kept his cap pulled low over his eyes as he hurried down the street and then into the construction zone. He crossed quickly under the cover of scaffolding, temporary walls, and construction debris until he exited into the airspace between the former grocery store and the building next door. Also owned by Deliverance shell companies, the six-story apartment building was undergoing renovations as well. Supposedly, anyway. He used a code to enter, then descended the stairs to the small basement before passing through a set of security doors to the operations center located in the concrete bowels.

Such precautions were probably not necessary, but Deliverance had remained completely anonymous for years, and part of its success lay in the strict rules and procedures that the team followed to the letter.

Dallas knew that.

He also knew that he was about to say a giant "fuck you" to those rules. He wanted Colin's head on a platter. He wanted answers.

He wanted them now, and the rules be damned.

He moved through the tech center, barely noticing Liam working at the computer while he spoke into a headset. No, his focus was entirely on the interrogation room as he moved in that direction with unfailing determination.

The door was shut and double-sealed, a clear indication that this was the room in which Colin was detained. Just to double check, Dallas glanced up at the video monitors, saw the man he'd once called friend sitting gagged in the single chair, his ankles lashed to the metal legs and his hands tied firmly behind his back.

"Dallas?" Liam's voice hardly registered. "Hold up, man."

But Dallas didn't even slow. Hell, he barely even broke his stride as he punched in the password, waited impatiently for the doors to open, then burst into the claustrophobic room and locked the door from the inside with his personal code.

A heartbeat later, his fist slammed hard into Colin's jaw, and the older man crashed backward onto the floor, chair and all.

Dallas straddled him, one hand twisting his collar as his other hand ripped off the gag, leaving Colin gasping, his eyes wide and unfocused.

"Dallas?" His voice seemed thin. Weak. "Thank god. Get me out of here. These men. They're—"

"Shut the fuck up." Dallas yanked him up, righting the

chair, then stood in front of the man who now cowered, as if sinking inside himself. "Who is she? The Woman? Who the fuck is she? And where the hell has she taken Jane?"

Colin's head shook as an almost incoherent string of denials escaped his lips. "I don't know what you're talking about. Please, Dallas, what's going on? Why are you here? Why am I here? I don't understand. Did something happen to Jane? Dallas, what's going on with my little girl?"

The words were spilling out of him, fast and furious. Pain and fear and regret seemed etched into every line of Colin's face, and for a moment—just a moment—Dallas hesitated. He wanted to believe that Colin was innocent. That his friend would never have hurt him. Would never have thrust Dallas and Jane into a concrete cell. Would never have starved and tortured them.

He wanted to believe, and that want felt like a fist around his heart.

But want couldn't overcome the truth, and Dallas had seen too much. Knew too much. His team had done their job, and the evidence was clear.

Dallas clenched his fists at his sides in an effort to calm the rage that writhed inside him like a caged beast. "Who. Is. She?" The words came out hard between clenched teeth.

"She?" Colin blinked, his forehead creased in concentration. "Jane?"

Dallas lashed out, his heart hurting as his palm connected hard and fast with Colin's cheek, sending the older man's head twisting to one side as he cried out in pain and surprise.

"The Woman, you fucking lowlife. The bitch who worked with you in London. The one who tortured us, who—"

The words caught in his throat, choking him, and he realized with a start that hot tears had pooled in his eyes. With a violent move, he kicked Colin's chair, then turned away, trying to gather himself. He couldn't lose it. Not now. Not when he needed answers so badly. When she was missing. When he had to find her. Had to save her.

He drew in a breath and turned back to the man. His captive now, not his friend.

He bent over, then placed his hands tight on Colin's shoulders, trapping the man and also controlling his own urge to lash out with his fists yet again. "Did you know we were closing in? Did you set the bitch on her? Did that vile excuse for a female take Jane so that you'd have leverage? Did the two of you plan it all out? Who the fuck is she, Colin? And where is she keeping Jane?"

"Dallas, Dallas, please. I don't understand. What's happened to Jane? I don't—I don't know what you're talking about. Oh, god. Oh, god, what's wrong with you? What are you doing?" He was crying now, his voice cracking as he pled. "I'd never hurt Jane. I'd never hurt you. You know that—how can you not know that?"

"You fucking liar. You goddamn psychopath. Did you really think you could just slide into our lives? Did you truly believe we'd never find out?"

"No, I—"

"Tell me," he demanded, and now his right hand moved to Colin's throat. "You tell me the truth right now—tell me where she is, tell me who the Woman is—or I swear this breath will be your last."

He squeezed and watched as Colin's eyes bulged. As his face turned red, then gray. As his mouth opened, not to speak, but to gasp for air that wasn't going to come. Dallas wanted to do it. Wanted to rip the last remnants of life from him, to destroy the man who had destroyed him and Jane. To punish the man who'd let that bitch torture him so many years ago, and who was surely now tormenting Jane.

He clenched harder, some part deep inside of him knowing that he had to let the man go, had to let him speak. But a larger part—a more powerful part—had taken over. He needed to take Colin out. He needed to end it. He needed to punish. To destroy.

He needed Jane.

And goddammit, he didn't know how to get her back.

"Dallas!" Strong hands grabbed his upper arms and ripped him backward, forcing his fingers off Colin's throat. "Rein it in, man. You can't kill him. We need him. We need him to find out who attacked Jane."

"He did." Dallas had to force the words out between gasps, he was breathing so hard. "Whether or not he was on the street, he's the one pulling the strings, just like always."

"Maybe." The rage was starting to fade from Dallas's ears. He recognized Liam's voice, and realized his friend used the override code to enter. "But do you think she'll forgive you if you kill him, especially if you kill him without letting her talk to him first?"

Liam's strong hands still held him firm, but Dallas whipped sideways, freeing himself, his fear that Jane was already dead driving him.

"The bastard deserves every ounce of pain I can give him. He deserves to starve. To rot. For what he did? He deserves to endure the worst we can give him." He met Liam's eyes. "How can you not understand that?"

He saw the pain and regret flash across his friend's face before he steeled himself again, then slowly shook his head. "I do," he said flatly. "Dammit, Dallas, you know what I lost. But you haven't lost Jane—not yet. She's alive," he continued, before Dallas could interrupt. "Did you hear me? Jane's alive."

The words sliced his legs out from under him, and Dallas crumpled, his knees no longer able to hold him up. "What?" he asked stupidly. "What are you saying?"

"I'm saying we've found her. Dallas, we've found Jane."

3

Sleeping Beauty

There is light, then pain. I'm confused—uncertain of where I am. Of *who* I am.

But then the world comes into focus, and I realize that this place feels safe. Good. I'd been fighting this awakening, this consciousness, because I feared what I would find when I opened my eyes. Dark, damp walls. A moldy mattress. A plastic bucket to use as a toilet. Stale crusts of bread to wash down with warm, brown water.

Instead, this room is welcoming. Simple, but filled with light. I am warm, not cold. And the woman beside me with tears in her eyes smiles at me with such love and tenderness that my fear and confusion fade; I have no room inside me for any emotion but joy.

This, I think. *This is what it feels like to be born.*

Dread replaced by wonder. Darkness swept away by light. And someone who loves you waiting at the end.

"Mommy?" The word feels like heaven against my dry, cracked lips.

"Jane! Oh, my sweet baby girl!" She clasps my hand and holds it tight. "Thank goodness you're awake!"

"What happened?" Only now do I look around, searching the rest of the room, panic rising once again as I glance toward the windows to my left, then back to my mother who stands on the other side of my bed, the closed door behind her. "Where's Dallas?"

It's hard to speak past the hard knot of fear that clogs my throat, but I have to hear that he is safe. Intellectually, I know that it's been seventeen years since we were locked in that filthy room. Seventeen years since we were cold and hungry, our passion our only reprieve from the horror. I know that—and at the same time, our kidnapping still feels fresh. Hard and cold and terrifying.

"He's right outside with Daddy." My mother's voice is calm. As soothing as her warm hands folded over mine. "They're talking to the doctors. They didn't expect you to wake up so soon. You have quite a few sedatives swimming in your blood."

That explains the muddle in my head, and I smile wryly at my mother. "It's like iocane powder," I say, referencing *The Princess Bride*, one of my favorite movies. "I've built up an immunity to every sedative imaginable."

I'm being flip, but maybe it's true. Over the years, I've taken a rainbow of pills to help me deal with the aftermath of the kidnapping. I haven't relied on them lately, though. I have Dallas now, the man who fills my heart and makes me whole. Who is so vital it seems at times as if we are two halves of the same person.

I look at the door with longing; I want to see him so badly it's like a physical ache. And yet at the same time I feel tense. Uncertain. And I don't understand why.

Frowning, I adjust the bed so that I'm sitting upright, hoping that will clear my fuzzy head. I try to think back. I remember waiting for him in the apartment, feeling safe even though

I knew that feeling wouldn't last. And I remember that we'd argued. But about what, I don't know.

I frown, looking up at my mother as I try to pull it all back. "Jane? Sweetheart."

"I can't remember. I know something happened—when? yesterday?—but I can't remember."

"You were attacked. Oh, baby, you were left unconscious on the street."

Her voice cracks, and her eyes leave my face, and I know my mother well enough to realize that if she continues to look at me, she's going to cry. I gently pull my hand free and hug myself. Because what she says feels true. I close my eyes, trying to remember.

I was outside, walking fast. I was upset, I'm sure of that, but I don't remember why.

I felt alone—so alone.

And then, suddenly, I wasn't alone anymore.

Someone was following me.

A shiver rips through me, and my eyes fly open. I stare up into my mother's concerned face. "There was a woman. Tall and thin and dressed all in red. And she had a mask."

"A carnival mask, yes," my mother says. "Like she was dressed for an old-fashioned masquerade."

I nod and lick my lips. "It was like . . . before." My mother must hear the shaking in my voice because she takes my hand and squeezes it tight as I look up at her. "It was her, wasn't it? The Woman? Was she the one who attacked me?"

Tears spill down my mother's cheeks, but she doesn't let go of my hand to wipe them away. "I don't know. Probably. Dallas thinks so. But there was a party that night. A masquerade at the natural history museum. It could have been a mugging. Or someone who doesn't like—"

"The fact that I'm sleeping with my brother?"

She winces. Just barely. And then she nods.

"Do you believe that?"

"I don't know, sweetie. I don't know what to think. Do you remember anything? Anything that might help us find whoever did this to you?"

I try to think, to pull some sort of key fact from my foggy memory, but there's nothing much there. "I know she had a Taser. I was walking, and I heard footsteps. Then when I turned around, it got me. Knocked me to the ground."

"Anything else?"

I nod, the movement making my head throb. "She had a stick—a club, I guess. The kind that extends. And she ... she ..."

I can't say it, but my hand goes to my face, and my mother gasps a little bit.

"Baby, oh, sweetheart."

My cheeks are wet, and I realize that I'm crying. "That's it," I say. "That's all I remember. The next thing I know, I was here." I swallow. "Do you know what happened to me?"

"Some. Dallas called us, of course. It's—it's horrible." She squeezes her eyes shut and shakes her head, as if whatever she is thinking is just too much.

"Mom?"

"They sent a picture of you to Dallas. On the sidewalk, I mean, and—oh, oh god."

"A picture?" I hear myself say the word, but I can't wrap my mind around what she means.

"A text message. From your phone. And he tracked your phone and went to you, but you weren't there." She sniffles and reaches for a tissue. "I just—if something worse had happened to you ..."

I reach out my hand for her. "I'm okay, Mom. I'm going to be fine."

She squeezes my fingers and nods, visibly gathering herself. "Somehow you ended up here and they admitted you as a Jane

Doe. Dallas had Liam and Quince helping from the moment he knew you'd been attacked, and when they found you'd been admitted, he rushed here and called me and Daddy on the way."

I nod. I know that Dallas would have told our parents I'd been attacked, but he wouldn't have told them about Deliverance. But they know that Liam is in security and Dallas's old boarding school roommate Quince is part of MI6, so my mom wouldn't find their help odd.

"Dallas." His name is soft on my lips, full of longing. I know he is just beyond those doors, so close I could walk to him, and yet at the same time he seems farther from me than he has ever been.

I still don't understand why I'm feeling that distance. I only know that it's there, hidden in my still-shadowed memory.

And then the door opens, and I watch as he enters, his long, purposeful strides underscoring the urgency of his movements. He is as tall and gorgeous as always, but today his caramel colored hair is wild and unkempt, as if he's spent hours unconsciously worrying it with his fingers. The angles of his sculpted face are more pronounced, the lines drawn from exhaustion, and it's clear he hasn't slept.

Remnants of fear cling to him like palpable things, but there is joy, too. And when he whispers my name, it's like a lifeline pulling us back together, making me whole. Making *us* whole.

I watch as a tentative smile touches his lips, as relief fills those vibrant green eyes. I could drown in the depths of emotion I see there, and I hold out a hand, needing to touch him. Needing to know that he's real.

He hurries to me, his throat moving as he swallows, and a tear snakes its way down his cheek as he clasps my hand in his.

It is as if his touch is an elixir, a magic potion that opens the doors of my memory, and I flinch. My heart pounds painfully in my chest, and I yank my hand free as memory floods through me, overwhelming me.

He opens his mouth to say something, but I beat him to it. *"Colin."*

It's the only word I speak, but as I do, memories rush back, hard and horrible. *Oh, god. Oh, god.* I remember now—I remember it all—and I look at Dallas, sure my eyes are full of harsh accusations.

He shakes his head, his face turning gray. "Jane—"

"He's trying, baby," my mother says, and we both turn to stare at her. "Your brother's been trying to get in touch with Colin to let him know what happened and that you're here. That you're okay."

"Has he?" I ask, shifting to look at Dallas again. I hear the edge in my voice. The bitter sarcasm. "I wonder why you haven't been able to find him."

I want to scream and rage and rant, and I know that Dallas can see that on my face.

"He must be traveling," my mother says, unaware of the silent recriminations passing from me to Dallas. "Jane, sweetie, lie back. I don't like your color. We need to get the nurse in to—"

"No." I force myself back against the pillow as my father steps into the room. "No, I'm feeling better. I'm just—I'm just so tired." I don't look at Dallas, but I know he understands me. I'm physically exhausted, yes. But that's not what I mean. I'm tired of the lies. Of the secrets.

I remember all the times I'd justified his secrets to myself because I knew he had stuff to deal with. All the times I'd asked him if he'd learned anything about our kidnapping. But never once had I suspected that he was keeping such a massive secret from me. That he would withhold his suspicion that Colin had been the Jailer. That Dallas would have the sheer audacity to suspect, capture, and incarcerate the man who started out as my birth father but became my friend.

I don't want to even think about the possibility that such a horrible thing is true, but Dallas should have told me. After all his promises, all his assurances that there would be no more secrets between us, he held back the one secret that ripped me to shreds and sent me running blindly from him, unable to process the depth of his deception. Unable to bear the weight of his lies.

And though I'd wanted him beside me just moments ago, now I want him to leave. Except I don't, because I want him to hold me. I want to go back in time. I want him to have never lied to me.

I want him.

I want us.

And I'm terrified that we've lost everything that we've built. That we've lost each other.

I draw a breath, then meet his eyes. "Go," I say. "Just, please, go."

Shadows haunt his eyes as he shakes his head. "Jane, no."

I turn to my mother, as if this is a simple argument between siblings and she needs to step in and play arbiter the way she did when we were kids.

But it's not my mother who answers, it's my dad, and I realize that I'd been so lost in the sight of Dallas that I hadn't noticed my dad's entrance. "She wants you to go," he says to Dallas. "Do your *sister* the courtesy of listening to her." The extra emphasis on the word "sister" makes us both cringe.

"Dad—" Dallas begins.

"This is your fault," my father snaps, his gravelly accusation directed solely at Dallas. "I hope you realize this is all on you. If you hadn't—back then, if you two hadn't—" He broke off, his voice raw, uneven. "If you'd only—"

"*Eli.*" My mother's voice is unusually harsh, and I watch as my father gathers himself, then looks at Dallas again, his expression blank.

"As I said, boy. She wants you to go."

"You, too, Daddy." My words are soft, but firm, because it is not only Dallas who has hurt and disappointed me, who has left the fabric of my world in tatters. "I need you to go, too."

For a moment, my father looks taken aback. Then he stands straighter. "Don't be ridiculous. You're upset and scared. But we need to know what you remember. Whoever did this to you—we have to find them."

Warm tears spill down my face. "I know. But not now. I didn't see anything, anyway. I just—I just want Mom." A hard sob sticks in my throat. "I can't handle anything else right now."

My father looks at me, this man who has been a powerhouse my entire life. He seems smaller now and a little lost. "Jane—baby girl—I love you."

"I believe you. I do. And if it's true, then I need you to do what I say I need, not what you want me to need. Both of you," I add with a glance toward Dallas.

For the first time in my memory, my father seems unsure of his course. Then my mother whispers, "Please, Eli, just for now."

Slowly, he nods. He takes a single step toward me, and I actually flinch. He freezes, his body tightening as if I'd reached out and slapped him. "I'm just—I'm just so damn glad you're okay."

Okay? I think. *Is that what I am? Okay?*

I say nothing, though, and he turns for the door. Dallas follows him, and I have to clench my hands to fight the urge to pull him back. I want him—I want him desperately—but the hurt is still too deep.

My father walks out without a backward glance, but Dallas pauses in the doorway, lingering there until I lift my head and meet his eyes. "I'm sorry," he says, and I look away, keeping my eyes on the floor as his footsteps fade down the hall and I wonder if I've just lost the two men I love most in all the world.

4

Revelations

I don't sleep. Instead, I drift, my thoughts in a fog, my body thick and unresponsive from the drugs. I feel tossed around, like a cork on a stormy sea.

No dreams fill my mind—no dark memories from the past, no terror that I will never wake again—and yet somehow that dark emptiness is even more disturbing than my usual nightmares simply because I can't get my bearings.

I am lost. Desolate. Alone.

Then I feel the gentle brush of a hand on my cheek, and it is like a lifeline, pulling me back, drawing me out of the storm.

A smile tugs at my lips—*Dallas*.

But then it fades as I remember that I sent him away. That I'm not ready to have him beside me. Not now. Not yet.

The hand I feel must belong to my mother. I open my eyes to reassure her that I'm okay, then jump when I see who is really touching me.

"Adele!" I jerk back, then push myself up to a sitting position, completely ignoring the buttons on this bed that would do that for me. "I—you startled me."

My family has been doing everything possible to ensure my privacy, including leaving me listed as a Jane Doe. My mom's even asked my best friend, Brody, not to come visit—though she did at least let him know what happened to me—because she's afraid some enterprising reporter will follow him to find me.

"I'm sorry," I stammer. "I'm just really jumpy."

"Of course you are," she coos. "You poor little thing." She presses a hand to my cheek, and a single tear traces a path down the side of her nose. "I just can't believe it."

I pull away, stretching to cover the motion. I don't want her touch. For that matter, I don't want anything from her. Maybe that's not fair, but I don't care. Right now, I'm too raw to care about propriety.

She seems entirely unaware of my hesitancy, because she continues to stand right beside me, fussing with the bedding, then dabbing at her eyes with a tissue. Adele is Colin's ex-wife, though they married when I was an adult, so even had Colin still been my legal father, I don't think I would ever have considered her my stepmother.

But it's not the relationship between Colin and Adele that puts me off. Instead, it's her past relationship with Dallas. I don't think she's aware that I know she slept with Dallas before he and I were together. But I do know that she's understood what Dallas and I are to each other for years, even before we revealed our secret to the press. And that fact makes me feel just a little bit too exposed.

"This city has just gone crazy," she clucks. "Attacked and left in Riverside Park like so much garbage." Her voice climbs with outrage. "Your mother told me all about it. I called her looking for Colin a few hours ago, and she told me the whole story."

The Deliverance guys have pieced together some of what happened, and Dallas relayed the chain of events to my mom. Well, *I* know it was the Deliverance guys. Mom thinks that Liam and Quince have pooled their resources. Which, in a way, they have.

Apparently, the woman who attacked me had an accomplice. A man who picked me up off the sidewalk and hauled me into the back of a white cargo van while the woman slid behind the wheel. The guys found three witnesses. A couple who were walking at the far end of the block and didn't realize what was going on until the van sped away. And a fourteen-year-old who was sitting by his window in one of the townhouses texting his girlfriend. He didn't see the attack. He didn't even see the man pick me up off the sidewalk. But he did see the bastard shoving me in the back, and then the van disappearing down the street.

But my assailants didn't bring me to the hospital. Instead, I was dumped—my veins pumped full of a narcotic cocktail—near one of the entrances to Riverside Park. Someone made an anonymous 911 call, and the paramedics whisked me away to the ER. None of which I remember, and the fact that I was completely unconscious and doped up on god-knows-what during all of that is more than a little freaky.

I pull the sheet up to my chest, feeling suddenly exposed. Adele doesn't seem to notice. She glances around the room, frowning.

"I expected Colin would be here," she muses.

"No," I say simply. "I haven't seen him."

"Well, that's odd. I just assumed your mother would have reached him by now. I'll start calling some mutual friends. Maybe he's tucked away in someone's hunting cabin or off on someone's yacht."

Before I have a chance to comment, my mother steps through the open door carrying two cups of coffee. "This stuff is as thick as sludge," Mom says, "but at least it's hot—oh! Adele!"

"Lisa, oh, Lisa." She deftly takes the Styrofoam cups from my mom and sets them on my hospital tray, then pulls my mom into an awkward hug. Awkward because my mother is as stiff as a board.

"Are you doing okay?" Adele asks once she's broken the embrace. "I know Jane is—I practically interrogated her attending before I came in here. But is there anything you need?"

Mom shakes her head and manages a smile, then looks between Adele and me. "Did I interrupt?"

I almost tell her that she did, just so she'll have an excuse to leave. Adele has never been on my mom's favorite-person list. Even though Mom's the one who walked away from Colin, I think she's always felt like Adele was an interloper.

But I just can't toss her that bone. I selfishly want her beside me, and so I shake my head. "We were just talking."

"Has Dallas been by?" Adele asks. "I assumed I'd see him here."

"He was right here when Jane woke up," my mom assures her.

"But he left?" Adele isn't even trying to keep the surprise out of her voice.

"I asked him to go," I admit, then immediately regret my words because I don't have an explanation for that. At least not one that I'm willing to share.

But Adele doesn't seem to need one. "That was smart. If he hangs around here, sooner or later the press will notice. An orderly will sneak a picture. And then you'll be all over Twitter. And you definitely don't need that."

"No," I agree. "I don't."

She looks between me and my mom, and though I have never thought of Adele as a soft person, right then her expression is almost maternal. "I'm going to leave you two alone. Jane, I'm so sorry this happened to you, and I'm so glad you're okay. You'll be released soon?"

"We're hoping for tonight," Mom says. "But as slow as the lab has been, it may be the morning."

"I'll keep my fingers crossed. And in the meantime, I'll go see Dallas. Let him know that you're okay. That you miss him," she adds, her lips curving in a small smile.

"You don't have to do that." I try to keep my voice light, even airy. Inside, I'm dying. I know there's nothing going on between Adele and Dallas anymore. And yet the thought of her being close to him makes me nauseous.

"Nonsense. Someone needs to check on him. Really, sweetie, it's no trouble at all." She blows me a kiss, gives my mom a hug, then strides out the door, her Jimmy Choos clicking on the floor as her Hermès Kelly handbag swings on her arm.

I lay back in my bed and draw in a deep breath, trying to steady myself. Trying to wrap my head around everything I'm feeling right now. The deep wound from Dallas's secrets about Colin. The sharp pain from Adele's casual familiarity.

Intellectually, I know that one has nothing to do with the other, but that doesn't matter. I want to scratch her eyes out.

More, I want Dallas right here, right now.

And I hate that weakness in me that craves Dallas even when he is the one who has made me hurt. Not the physical hurt of the attack, but the emotional hurt of the betrayal.

"I've always thought that woman was something of a bitch, bless her little heart."

I stare at my mom, see the twinkle in her eye, and burst out laughing.

"She's okay," I say, because I know damn well my mother has no clue that there was ever anything sexual between Dallas and Adele. "She just pokes her nose in where it isn't wanted."

"And you want Dallas here," Mom says. "Not with her."

I only shrug, neither admitting nor denying.

"Hmmm," she says in that way she has. She pulls up a chair and sits next to the bed. "You know," she begins conversationally, "I really do understand why you're upset with your father. Disinheriting you both, and so publicly. I imagine you're just as mad at me."

"No," I assure her, a little flummoxed by this sudden shift in the conversation. "I get it—I know Daddy. It's not like we didn't expect him to cut us off. So I'm not mad, not really. Not at Daddy. Not at you." I lick my lips and look up at her. "But I am . . ." I trail off with a shrug. "Disappointed?"

Frowning slightly, she picks up her coffee cup, then gently blows at the surface of the hot liquid. "I'm disappointed in myself, too," she says after a moment. "But that's not what I meant. I'm just saying that I understand why you're upset with your father and me. But I don't understand what happened between you and Dallas."

"Nothing happened," I lie.

The corners of her mouth tighten slightly. "When you sent him away, I thought it was because it was just too much. Because you needed some Mom time." Her smile is gentle. "But this isn't about me at all, is it?"

I consider perpetuating my lie a little bit longer, but I can't stand tossing yet another deception into the mix. "It's not," I finally admit, and I try to find the words to tell her the truth about Dallas's betrayal. About the huge secret he kept and how deeply it wounded me. If anyone would understand, she would, because although she and Colin have been divorced for years and years, I know that part of her still loves him, despite all the ways he hurt and disappointed her.

But I can't tell her.

I sit there in my hospital bed, my head bursting with one singular absolute—*I flat-out can't tell her.*

She's already been through so much with him, and if she

knew that there was even the tiniest possibility that Colin—a man she was married to, a man with whom she fathered a child—was the instigator behind the kidnapping of me and Dallas seventeen years ago . . .

Well, if she knew that, it would break her. She could never un-know it. And even if we never learn for certain who the kidnapper really was, the possibility it might be Colin would haunt her forever.

So I can't tell her. I can't do that to her. Not until I'm certain. Not and live with myself.

And that's when it hits me—that's when I finally understand what Dallas did. And, more importantly, why.

"Sweetie?" my mom presses. "Are you okay?"

I realize that I have pulled the covers up to my chin. "I'm fine," I lie. "I'm just so very tired."

Even as I speak, I realize it's true. Exhaustion is carrying me away like a riptide, threatening to pull me down into the black.

"Tell him," I whisper before I succumb. "Tell him for me."

"Tell him?" my mother asks. "Tell him what?"

But the weight of sleep is too much, and I can't speak the words that ring through my head. *I love him, Mommy. Tell Dallas that I love him.*

5

Lost Without You

It was two-fifteen in the morning, and Dallas couldn't sleep. He poured another glass of bourbon, knowing damn well it would do nothing, and tossed it back.

The liquor burned his throat and clouded his head, but that's what he wanted. Punishment and forgetfulness. To just fucking erase all of it.

Not possible though, and so he turned to alcohol to take the edge off. And right then, there were a lot of goddamn edges.

Fuck.

Liam had rightfully pulled him away from Colin, then Jane had rightfully sent him away from her. He didn't have a place with the man he now despised, and he didn't have a place with the woman he loved.

He was alone and he was drunk and he couldn't sleep and the whole situation was just too goddamned fucked up for him to wrap his head around.

A soft tap at the door startled him, and he cringed. *Adele.*

Goddammit, he'd told her he didn't want to see her when she'd called earlier to tell him she'd visited Jane. "She's doing well, but I worry about you two. Are you sure you're prepared for this? Living in the spotlight?"

"I've always been in the spotlight," he'd countered.

"Not like this."

He'd almost tossed back a sarcastic comment—something about how his sex life had always been front and center. But she was right. This was different. With Jane, he wasn't in the spotlight because he was a player, but because of who he was playing with.

"And it's not just the fact that you're sleeping with your sister," Adele had continued. "Eventually they'll find out what happened between you two. Innocent children trapped in a horrible situation, and they'll make it seem dirty."

"It won't come out."

"I hope you're right," she'd said. "But secrets have a way of being discovered."

She'd told him she was on her way over to keep him company, but he'd shut that down quickly. But Adele was Adele, and apparently she'd decided to come anyway, probably bribing the doorman to let her into the elevator.

"Dammit, Adele," he said as his hand closed over the knob. "I told you I didn't want you to—*Jane.*"

She was wearing hospital scrubs, and her hair was pulled back into a messy ponytail. The bruise on her cheek had turned a sick shade of yellow, and the dark circles under her eyes were large enough to get lost in.

She looked exhausted, shattered.

She looked beautiful.

He wanted to pull her into his arms, but he forced himself to stay still, not sure where this moment was leading, but praying that it was leading her back to him.

Right then, her hands were deep in her pockets, and she lifted one shoulder in a small shrug. "I don't have a key. For that matter, I don't have a purse."

"You don't need one," he said, stepping aside even as he made a mental note to change the lock. "Come in."

Her teeth grazed her lower lip as she crossed the threshold, her eyes darting quickly to his face and then back again. God, they were being so tentative with each other, and that awkwardness was killing him.

"How did you get past all the reporters camped outside?"

An actual smile flickered. "I guess they work bankers' hours. There was only one guy out there, and he didn't even look twice at me." She gestured to her scrubs. "Maybe he figured I was a doctor coming home late."

"Still, it was a risk coming here alone. There might have been more. They might have recognized you. Mobbed you."

"Some risks you have to take." She lifted her head, met his eyes. "Don't you?"

He couldn't take it any longer. He'd even shoved his hands into his pockets so that he wouldn't reach out and touch her. "Jane. Please. Why are you here?"

For a moment, she looked confused. Then a single tear spilled down her cheek. "Oh, god, Dallas. Where else would I be?"

"I don't know. With Brody. In a hotel. Anyplace but here with me."

"Did you think I could leave you? Really? Ever? Don't you know what we are to each other?" She flashed a mischievous smile. "Haven't you been paying attention?"

"I thought I'd screwed it up."

Again, she lifted a shoulder. "You did." She took a step toward him, and it was all he could do not to pull her closer, to hold her tight. "You did," she repeated. "And you didn't."

He tilted his head, afraid to get his hopes up. "What are you saying?"

"I'm saying I love you," she said, her words filling his heart. "And I understand why you didn't tell me."

He tilted his head slowly to the side, surprised by this second simple statement. "Do you?"

She licked her lips, then told him about her conversation with their mom. About how Lisa was worried about Colin. "I wanted to tell her," Jane concluded. "I thought she deserved to know what you say he did. But I couldn't."

Her eyes were wet with tears. "She was so worried about why no one was able to find Colin, and I couldn't say a word to her. Because even the slightest hint that he had anything to do with our kidnapping would have killed her." With a sigh she shoved her hands into the pockets of her scrubs. "She would have blamed herself. She would have second-guessed her decision to marry him in the first place. Every decision she made over a huge chunk of her life. So I couldn't tell her. Not yet, anyway."

He stared at her, and then, very slowly, he nodded. "You do get it."

"Yeah, well, I'm still pissed."

"I wouldn't do it any differently if I had to do it all over again," he admitted.

"I know. I told you I get it. Just tell me one thing."

"Anything," he said, and he meant it.

"Are you absolutely certain about Colin? You have evidence? Solid evidence?"

"I told you we did." He spoke gently, because he knew the truth hurt her. But at the same time, he wasn't willing to sugar-coat it.

She nodded, hugging herself. "That's what you said before. I believe you—hell, I believed you then. But I don't want it to be true."

He moved closer, then gently tugged her hands free from her pockets and held them in his. "Do you want me to tell you?"

"I—no. I mean, yes. I have to hear it all. I know that. It's just . . ." She trailed off, then met his eyes. "There are so many things to say. Important things. Essential things."

"Jane—"

"But not now. I don't want to talk about any of it right now."

Hope warred with fear inside him.

"I just want—oh, please, Dallas. I don't want to talk. Right now, I just want you to kiss me."

And that was it—that was the moment she broke him. He felt himself shatter, the fear that had hardened inside him like glass breaking into a million tiny pieces. He reached for her, then cupped her head and closed his mouth gently over hers.

Immediately, he became drunk on the taste of her, aroused by the feel of her.

He wanted to crush her body against his, to feel her heat, her heart. He wanted to bruise her mouth with his kisses and close his hands tight around her arms. He'd come so damn close to losing her, and he couldn't stand the thought of ever letting her go.

But he didn't—he couldn't. She was too fragile, and the possibility that he might hurt her—more, again—ate at him. So instead, he littered soft kisses on her face, her neck. He stroked her. Touched her. Hell, he worshipped her.

"Dallas?" Tentatively, her fingers brushed his face.

He blinked and focused on a space over her shoulder, knowing that he'd come completely undone if he looked into her eyes. "I thought I'd lost you. First, when you walked out. And then—and then—"

The words caught in his throat, too horrible to even voice. "Christ, Jane. I can't lose you."

Gently, her fingertip stroked his lower lip. Even more gently, she took his chin and forced him to look at her. "I'm right here."

"And thank God for that."

Their eyes met and held, and for a moment there was no time, no space, no world that judged them. There was just them.

Then she lunged, her mouth closing over his with such firm finality that it both broke the moment and had him laughing. "This is how I want you," she said, and he answered her silently but enthusiastically, pulling her hard against him, slamming his mouth against hers. Taking. Consuming. Until he was nothing but heat and need, an ache building in him that he couldn't quench no matter how tight he held her, how hard he kissed her.

He was lost in her, drowning in the sensuality of her fingernails digging into his back. Of her teeth claiming his lips. Of the way her pelvis ground hard against his erection.

With a low, needful groan, he slid his hands down and grabbed her hips, craving an even closer contact. He tightened his grip, pulled her toward him, then immediately released her and stepped back when she released a soft, sharp, "Oh!"

"Jane?"

She stood before him, breathing hard. "I'm sorry, I'm sorry."

He frowned. "I hurt you."

"No. No, I'm fine." She shook her head, but he knew better. "Dallas, please. I don't want—"

"What?"

"Distance." She dragged her teeth over her lower lip as if she was unsure about how he felt.

"Oh, baby. No. Never." He held out his hand. "Come here."

She cocked her head, then narrowed her eyes. "Where?"

"Do you trust me?"

"Yes."

The speed of her reply sang in his heart. "Then let me take care of you."

The corner of her mouth twitched. "If you're thinking about putting me to bed, you can just stop that nonsense right now.

I've been in a hospital for almost two days. Between boredom and sedatives, I'm all caught up on my sleep."

"I promise, sleep is the last thing on my mind."

That was a little bit of a lie. She'd protest, he knew, but she needed more sleep. Good sleep, not with nurses popping in and out and a sterile bed with the scent of hospital disinfectant permeating the room.

She'd sleep, all right. But he intended to make sure she was ready for it. That she would drift under, safe and warm and content in his arms.

Gently, he drew her into the bathroom, her favorite room in the apartment. The previous owners had knocked out a wall, turned the small second bedroom into a closet, and used part of that space to make room for a steam shower and an oversize whirlpool tub. The day they'd moved in, Jane had told him this bathroom was a little slice of heaven.

He turned the water on, cranking up the heat the way he knew she liked it, then he stood her on the dense, white rug that filled most of the space.

"Are you tending me?" Her voice was as teasing as her expression, and it was all he could do not to gather her close and sigh with contentment. Yes, he knew she was still aching and sore. No, they didn't know who her attacker was. Yes, her birth father was locked in a cell, and Dallas was the one keeping him there.

But none of that mattered. Not then. All he cared about—all he could hold in his head—was Jane. That she was alive. That she was his.

That she'd come back to him.

"Damn right I'm tending you. Now put your hands up," he added with mock sternness.

She complied, and he peeled off her scrub top, delighted to find that she wore nothing beneath it. Her breasts were perfect, round and firm, and as he watched, her nipples tightened and her areolae puckered. He wanted to roll her nipples between his fingers. He wanted to taste her breasts and feel her arch back and moan, her tits hard and hot in his hands as he licked and sucked, taking her so far that she came in his arms simply from the pressure of the desire building between her legs.

Not now. Not yet.

Instead, he met her eyes. Then he lowered his gaze to her chest, watching it rise and fall as her desire heightened to match his. Her pulse quickened in her throat, another spot that he wanted to lick and tease.

Slowly, he reached for the drawstring of her pants. His fingers brushed her abdomen as he did, the touch so light it was almost negligible. It was enough, though, and he felt the shock of that connection all the way down to his cock. He was rock hard and straining against his jeans. And when her pants slid over her hips to the floor—when she stood before him completely naked—he had to fight the battle of his life not to step forward, slide his hand between her thighs, and feel the creamy heat of her arousal.

Instead, he simply stood and stared and wanted, his gaze caressing her. Reviewing every curve, every nuance. He knew her body as well as he knew his own, and the bruises he saw on her thighs and hips started a slow burn inside him.

He was going to kill whoever did this. No doubt. No question.

"Dallas."

Her voice drew him back.

"I'm okay. I'm safe, and I'm here, and I don't want to think about it."

Reluctantly, he nodded. He should have known she'd read his mind.

"Really," she urged, then grinned mischievously. "Need me to prove it?" As she spoke, she slid her palm down over her ribs, her belly, then between her thighs. She made a whimpering noise, and he almost exploded right then.

"Oh, no you don't."

She lifted a shoulder in a casual shrug. "No? But it feels so good. Are you going to make me a better offer?"

"Damn right," he said, then scooped her off her feet, shocking her into laughter.

Christ, but he wanted to take her. He wanted to claim her like a fucking caveman. Wanted to lose himself inside her and thrust hard and deep until she cried out his name. Until she drew blood with her fingernails, marking him as belonging to her.

He wanted wild heat and violent passion. He wanted to feel everything there was to feel, and then take it up tenfold from that.

He wanted all of that and more—but right now he couldn't have it. Because what he wanted even more was to care for her. To push his own needs aside and tend to her. He'd give her what she wanted, absolutely. But not in the way she expected.

Careful not to press too hard on her various bruises, he gently deposited her in the half-full tub. Then he opened the bottle of bubble bath she'd unpacked first thing, and added two capfuls. The smell of lavender infused the room, and she breathed in deep, then sighed. "You joining me in here?"

"I'm not," he said, then chuckled at her surprised expression. "Now lean back, close your eyes, and let me take care of you."

She sat back, but she didn't shut her eyes. Instead, she reached out for him, twining her bubble-clad fingers with his as she looked so deep into his eyes it seemed as if she'd crawled into his soul. "You've always taken care of me."

Her voice was a whisper, low and intense. It rumbled through him, pushing away the last bits of doubt, the lingering fear that she hadn't fully come back to him.

"I have," he said, the simple words belying the way his heart swelled in his chest. "And I always will."

6

Inevitable

"Oh, god, Dallas, yes." I'm leaning back against a bath pillow, my mind drifting from the scent of lavender even as my senses fire from the temptation of his hands on my heated body.

I'm still sore—my muscles tight and my bruises tender—but those aches are nothing compared to the burning need that Dallas's touch is driving within me. I don't care about the pain or the stiffness or the exhaustion that seems to pull me down like weights sinking in a churning ocean. All I want is his touch. All I care about is that I am back in his arms.

I know that he can tell how desperate I am. How could he not? This is the man who anticipates my needs. Who knows me at least as well as I know myself. And there is no way that he can miss the desire that I know is so palpable it must be wafting off my body like perfume.

I crave his body against mine. I long for wildness. For heat. For bone-melting passion.

And yet it doesn't come.

Instead, he teases me with soft touches and gentle strokes,

and I moan softly, biting my lip to keep from begging as his fingertip traces up and down my arm, the sensual rhythm soothing me even as it stokes the embers of my growing passion.

I know what he is doing—he is tending me. Coddling and protecting me. I can feel the tension in his touch, a tightness that underlies the slow and easy sensuality of his caresses. He wants to lose himself in the fire as much as I do, and yet he's holding back. Reining in his own desire in order to pamper me.

But, dammit, I want more than just gentle touches. And though I say nothing, I shift my body, arching my back so that my breasts rise out of the water in a not-so-subtle hint. I want to feel everything building inside me, and then, dammit, I want to explode.

Dallas, however, steadfastly refuses to satisfy me. Instead, he continues his leisurely assault. Fingertips tracing from my shoulder to my wrist. His lips brushing my forehead, his tongue teasing my ear. I feel a throbbing demand between my thighs, and I can't hold back any longer. "Please. Dallas, please."

He says nothing, but the lazy progression of his fingers shifts direction, slipping easily up my arm to caress my shoulder, careful to avoid the still red and tender scrapes from where I fell back on it. Slowly, his fingers tease down toward my breasts. So slowly that I can hardly stand the anticipation, and I hold my breath, waiting for that sweet moment when his finger will caress my nipple.

He draws out the torment—and the pleasure. Slowly, he cups my breast, slipping his hand into the water before bringing his dampened fingers out to toy with my nipple, rolling it between his thumb and forefinger as I bite my lip and moan, losing myself in the fiery pleasure now throbbing between my legs.

"Do you like that?" His lips brush my ear as he speaks, and a flurry of sparks course through me.

"Yes. Oh, god yes."

"Tell me what you want."

"You. More. Please." I have been reduced to single syllables, and I slide my hand down beneath the bubbles and between my legs.

Gently he reaches under the water, takes my wrist, and tugs my hand away. "Oh, no, baby. That's for me."

"Then touch me, dammit."

"Whatever the lady wants," he says, his low voice rumbling with amusement. He stands, moving forward a bit so he's now in my field of vision. His jeans and T-shirt are damp, but he doesn't seem to notice. As for me, all I'm noticing is that he's no longer touching me, and I whimper in protest.

A slow grin plays across his mouth as he leans over to turn the taps back on. The tub has a handheld nozzle, and as he lifts it from its hook, he orders me to stand up, then flips the toggle to drain the tub.

I shiver a bit now that I'm out of the tub, but Dallas soon aims the gentle spray over my body, warming me and sending clusters of bubbles sliding down my skin to melt in the tub before swirling down the drain. He's thorough in his washing of me, aiming the spray at my shoulders, then down the curve of my back. He circles around and concentrates on my breasts, then slowly moves the nozzle down and down until the spray is gently teasing between my thighs. With a little gasp, I spread my legs, wanting more.

He doesn't disappoint, and I release an impassioned moan when he aims the spray at my clit, then reaches between my legs with a cloth to carefully cleanse me, the friction making my core clench tight. I close my eyes, then reach blindly for the towel bar, wanting to steady myself for the storm I know is coming.

Except it doesn't.

I open my eyes, confused.

"Not just yet," he says.

Bastard.

"In that case, I may as well get out." I start to reach for the towel, but he beats me to it.

"Tonight, I'm taking care of you." Slowly—gently—he eases the towel over my body, drying me off, and, in the process, igniting my senses even more. I know it's intentional, and I bite my lip so as to not beg for a more intimate touch. I already know damn well he's not going to touch me until he's ready. And I know that he wants me to beg.

Right now, I'm determined to practice the art of self-control.

I manage for a while. My breath is shaky as he strokes the towel over my breasts, then slides it behind my neck before easing it between my legs. I sigh when he finally wraps me, warm and soft and safe, in the thick terry cloth, then lifts me effortlessly into his arms.

I snuggle against him as he carries me to the bedroom. It's still a mess, filled with open boxes, books, papers, and clothes piled up in corners. He sits me on the edge of the bed, then brushes the hair off my face. I feel like a child, being soothed after a bad dream, and yet there is nothing childlike about the way his touch makes me feel.

"Dallas," I say, and it's all that I say. But I know he hears the plea in my voice.

He bends and kisses me, sweet and gentle and so full of emotion that it makes me gasp. Makes my heart constrict.

He breaks the kiss and meets my eyes, and though I know him almost as well as I know myself, I can't read what I see there. I start to ask, but his finger on my lips silences me.

He takes my towel away, then eases me back so that I am stretched out on the bed. Slowly, he kisses me down my body, and I slip into a state of bliss, my head on the soft feather pillow, my body floating in space as his lips and hands trail gently over my breasts, my belly, my thighs.

I shift, parting my legs, not even trying to be coy about where I want those kisses next, but that touch doesn't come. Instead, I feel the cool brush of material moving up my body.

With a frown, I open my eyes and see that he is pulling up the crumpled sheet to cover me.

"You need rest," he says in response to the astonishment that surely covers my face.

"The hell with that. I need you."

"You have me. Always. I can't believe there was a time when we fought it, because I can't live without you."

The intensity of his voice breaks through me, and my throat feels suddenly thick with tears. "Me neither." I may have walked away from him before the attack, but I could never have stayed away. We're bound, he and I. We're inevitable. And despite the taboo, those binds between us don't feel like chains, but like a gift. Because how many people actually find the one person in all the universe with whom they can fully share themselves?

"Then sleep," he says as he sits on the edge of the bed beside me and strokes my hair. "I'm not going anywhere. Let me take care of you."

"Then do it. Take care of me." I take his hand and guide it beneath the sheet to my breast, then arch back against his palm. I want him so bad I am aching. And while I know that he feels like he needs to coddle me, right now I need more.

"Letting me sleep isn't helping me," I insist. "Letting me sleep is ignoring me. Dallas, please. Please," I repeat as I slowly guide his hand down over my ribs, my belly.

His eyes are on mine, all dark heat and wild desire. But there's something else, too. He's still holding back, still second-guessing what he thinks is best for me.

"This," I say as I spread my legs and guide him lower, trailing his fingers over my smooth pubic bone and then lower still to cup my sex. "Touch me," I say. "Fuck me," I beg.

Electricity shoots through me, and I quiver, closing my eyes as I arch up and manipulate his fingers to tease my clit.

"Oh, Christ, baby." His words are low and hard, almost a growl, and I know that I have him.

"Bye-bye sleep," I murmur as he eases two fingers inside me even as he bends forward to take my breast in his mouth.

He moves over me and lowers his mouth to my breast. His teeth graze my nipple, and I cry out, bucking against him as he nips and bites, then kisses his way down my body. He pauses at my pubic bone, then tilts his head up to look at me. "Is this what you want? My mouth on your pussy? My tongue teasing your clit while I thrust my fingers deep inside you?"

My body clenches in response to his words, and I manage a garbled sound that is reasonably close to a yes.

"I'm going to take you to the edge, baby. Right to the edge, but not over. Not yet."

I whimper, then almost beg, but his tongue flicking over my clit silences me, and I arch up, the pleasure almost too much to bear. But he won't let me escape any of the delights with which he torments me. Instead, he holds my hips firmly in place as his tongue works a wild magic on me. I'm close, so close, and my breath is shallow as I focus on that one spot, that one place where all the pleasure in the world seems to be trapped, and Dallas is so close to releasing it, and if he would just—

But then he stops, and I'm left on the precipice. I cry out in frustration, but as I do, he releases my hips and thrusts his fingers inside me. My body clenches around him and I almost cry with relief.

I need this so much. No, not this. *Him.* I've missed him. Hell, I've missed us. And the feeling of him inside me is like coming home. "More," I whisper. "Dallas, please, more. Everything. *You.*"

I'm not even coherent, but I know he understands.

Even so, he backs away from me, and I'm about to call him every dirty name I know, when I realize that he's not leaving. On the contrary, he's stripping, peeling off the damp jeans and then tossing his shirt across the room. He stands there for a moment, naked and perfect, his cock hard and ready. Just seeing him makes my body respond, my pussy clenching in anticipation of him filling me. *He's mine.* And right now, I want him inside me.

More than that, I want it hard. Fast. I want the wildness of being claimed. The surrender of being filled. And I'm completely shameless when I beg him, "Please, please, please, just fuck me." The words rush out of me without thought, and it's only after their echo has lingered that I think how wonderful it is that I can make that demand. For so long, Dallas hadn't been able to penetrate a woman, and I'd feared I'd never feel him inside me again.

But we're mostly past that now. Not one hundred percent, but pretty damn close.

Right now, though, he's not inside me, even though he's moved back to the bed. And I'm starting to realize that unless he's changed his approach to sex, he's totally not going in that direction.

"Dammit, Dallas, what are you doing?" I ask when he lifts his head from between my legs and aims a slow, sexy smile at me. "Or rather, what is your tongue doing and your cock *not* doing?"

His low laughter seems to rumble through me. "I told you, baby. Tonight is all about you."

"Then do what I ask and fuck me. Please," I add, then reach down and grab his hair so that he has no choice but to slide up my body when I tug. "You won't hurt me," I whisper, then lightly kiss the corner of his mouth. "Or if you do, I promise I'll enjoy it."

I can tell by the twitch of his lips and the gleam in his eye that any additional argument he puts up will be only for show. And when he lowers his head and slides down my body, I tremble and spread my legs wider, relishing the feel of him, the touch of him. And losing myself in the anticipation of what is to come.

Roughly, he grabs my thighs, tugging me down the bed as he wraps my legs around his hips. My sensitive pussy rubs against his cock and I arch up, my body aching for more.

"Fuck, yes," he says, and there's no longer any humor in his voice. Just need. Desperation. The tip of his cock teases me, sliding over my clit, dipping inside me just enough that I almost cry out in frustration.

I squirm against him, pleasure rising in my body, electricity swirling in my belly and between my legs. I clench the sheet and shift my hips as his cock strokes my clit.

"Please, Dallas. I'm begging. Now, please, *now*."

He growls an unintelligible response and then grasps my hips, pulling me toward him as he thrusts forward. I'm desperately wet, and he enters me deep in one hard, violent thrust that has me crying out as he fills me, then pulls out and slams into me again.

It's hard and hot and wild and exactly what I wanted even though with each tug on my hips he slides me down the sheet, irritating my abraded shoulder. But I don't care. On the contrary, I relish the pain. It underscores the moment, marking the return of a reality in which I belong to Dallas, wholly and completely. Because the pain means that I'm here.

The pain means that I'm alive.

And I never feel more alive than in Dallas's arms.

Again and again he thrusts inside me. "I'm close," he says. "Touch yourself, baby. I want to watch you play with your clit—and I want you to come with me."

"Yes." It's the only word I can manage, but I obey. I slide my fingers down, then brush against his cock as I stroke myself. It's wildly erotic, and a shudder rips through me, pushing me closer to the edge and then, yes, all the way over so that I cry out, my body tightening convulsively around his cock, taking him all the way, too, so that we both explode at the same time.

I swear I see stars, and when I finally come back to earth, he is on the bed on top of me, and we are both breathing hard. "Oh, baby," he murmurs, then eases over so he doesn't crush me. "I love you," he says, and to me his voice sounds like it's underscored by chimes.

Chimes?

And then it's not chimes that I hear, but Dallas's low curse as he bolts off the bed and rips into his jeans pocket in search of his phone.

I prop myself up on my elbows. I'm about to give him shit for his lack of sexy time manners, but then I see the expression on his face.

"That's Liam," he says, and meets my eyes. And in that second, I feel a shift. Neither of us know what Liam is going to say, but we both know it won't be good, and that this sweet, warm moment is about to evaporate completely.

I sit all the way up and reach for Dallas, then hold his wrist as he answers the call.

"Jane's with me. You're on speaker. What's happened?"

"We were working on Jane's phone when it received a series of texts."

For a minute, I'm confused. What's the big deal about my phone getting some texts? Then, of course, my stomach twists and knots.

I get it.

I understand.

"She sent them," I say. "The bitch who attacked me."

"Forward them," Dallas orders.

"Doing that right now," Liam says, and only seconds later, Dallas's phone dings to signal incoming text messages. Dallas opens the app and bile rises in my throat as I see the words that pop up on the screen:

Dallas, I could have done so much worse. I didn't, because I knew it would upset you.

But that's not really fair, is it? Because you've upset me.

How can you be with her when you should be with me? How can you touch her when you should be touching me?

I can forgive you because I love you, and you deserve a second chance.

But I will only bend so far before I break.

I know you don't really love her—how could you when I am the one who fills your heart? Who belongs at your side?

But maybe you do care for her. She's your sister. She's family. And you two shared a traumatic past.

You see? I understand and forgive. To a point.

So if you care for her, leave her.

Because the next time I meet her on the street, I'll truly end this. I have to, my love. How else can I protect what is mine?

I read the words once, twice. I know that Dallas will do everything he can to protect me. I know that Liam and Quince and the rest of the Deliverance guys are doing everything they can to find my attacker.

But I also know that she's whacked. That she truly thinks that Dallas is hers.

And that she has just flat-out sworn to kill whoever stands between them.

"Whoever," of course, is me.

7

Truth Deceives

"That. Fucking. Bitch." Dallas's voice is cold and hard and even. If I weren't already scared by the damn text, his tone alone would have terrified me. "Track it," he says to Liam. "Find her."

And then he hangs up. Just ends the call. He tosses the phone across the bed. It slides off, and lands with a thud on the carpeting. As far as I can tell, he doesn't even notice.

Slowly, he stands. Paces. He's like a caged cat, and it's only when I realize that I've slid backward in the bed and have pulled my knees up to my chest and am holding the sheet under my chin that I realize just how on the edge I am from watching him. *Not a cat,* I think wildly. *A spring, wound tight.*

And even as that metaphor enters my head, the explosion I'd been anticipating comes. He topples the armchair in the corner. He sweeps his arm over the dresser, sending small boxes flying. He puts his fist through the drywall beside the closet door.

But when he heads into the bathroom, I race after him, terrified that he'll punch the mirror and slice himself to ribbons.

"Dallas, don't!"

I catch him right on the threshold, and he whips around to look at me. In the same motion, he grabs my shoulders and slams me back against the wall. For an instant, I see the wild fury in his eyes. Not at me, but at the world.

And then I can't see his eyes at all, because he's too close, his mouth hot on mine. He breaks the kiss just long enough to yank my arms above my head, then holds them there, his hand cupping my wrists even as his mouth slams hard against mine.

He needs this—I know he does. And, dammit, so do I. The feel of him against me. The safe reality that it is Dallas touching me. Not fear. Not the world. And definitely not the Woman.

I want what he is taking, this demanding, heated longing. This passionate assault.

And yet despite my desperation, I can't handle it. I'm too sore, my body still too battered, and though I try to hold it back, I whimper as my abraded shoulder sings with pain, and he immediately shuts down, his anger buried fast and completely by his concern for me.

It's such a simple thing, and yet it fills me with so much joy that I wrap my arms around him and kiss him tenderly.

When we break the kiss, he looks at me softly, his hands stroking my hair. "You're mine, Jane. Don't ever leave me again."

There's a hardness in his words, but I know it's not meant for me. This isn't really about me walking away. It's his challenge to a fucked-up universe. It's his threat to the Woman. It's his way of telling me and the world that he can't bear to lose me again.

And though I understand all of that, the answer that comes to my lips is simple and personal. I look into his eyes and say softly, "Don't ever lie to me again."

He steps back, his hands dropping to his sides. "You're still angry."

"No. Maybe a little." I frown, because I'm honestly not sure. "Does it matter?" I ask. "The bottom line is, I love you."

"Say that again."

I raise my hand and cup his cheek in my palm. He hasn't shaved today—maybe not even since yesterday—and his face feels scratchy against my skin. "I love you," I say, and I watch as my words light his face. And then I frown as I see the shadow touch his eyes.

"Dallas?"

"I was so goddamn scared of losing you."

I swallow, then nod. I know that he's talking not only about the attack, but about the way I stormed out of our apartment. But that one's not a real fear, because we both know that I could never have stayed away. Not really. I tried before, after all, and I failed. Thank god, I failed, because now I'm with Dallas.

But the other fear—that I will be taken from him—is real, and it terrifies me, too.

I tilt my head to look up at him, wishing that he would say consoling things. That he would begin talking and tell me that it's all going to be okay, that there is no one out there to hurt me. But that's not going to happen. I have to face this. And I'm so damn grateful that I don't have to face it alone.

"You really think it was the Woman, don't you." My words are a question, but I already know the answer.

"How much did you see? Did you see her wearing the mask?"

I nod. "But it could have been anyone," I add lamely. "That text could have come from someone who thinks that killing me would erase some horrible sin."

"Could be, but it wasn't. And you know it wasn't."

I nod again. I know the truth. I just want to wrap myself tight in a warm blanket of denial.

"We have to find her. We have to keep you safe."

I close my eyes, then simply breathe. "She could have killed me then. She said so in that damn text. Why didn't she?"

"You know why."

He's right. I do. "She's playing with us." I mull over my own words, not sure how to say this, but knowing that I owe him the truth. "I'm scared," I admit. "I don't want to be, but I am. And that pisses me off, because that bitch already took too much from me. I don't want to give her my peace of mind, too."

"Jane." He reaches for me, but I turn away, not yet finished.

"I'm scared," I repeat. "But it's not just for myself. You're the one she's really after. You're the one she's going to want to hurt."

"But, baby, you're missing the point. She *does* want to hurt me. And she knows that the surest way to do that is to go through you."

His words chill me, and I hug myself and nod. He's right, of course. Dear god, he's absolutely right.

I take a deep breath and force myself to think rationally. "She thinks there's something between you two and I'm the thing that's keeping you apart."

"There's not. You're not."

That actually makes me smile. Almost. I tilt my head back, take a deep breath, and say, "Well, duh." Then I press on. "But what's going to happen when she's forced to realize that? It's going to be bad, Dallas. We have to find out who she is."

"Believe me when I say we're working on that."

I nod, understanding that *we're working on it* means *Quince* is working on it. Or more accurately, Quince is working on Colin.

I draw in a breath. "I need to see him."

"Jane—no."

There's a tightness to his voice that I know is worry, but I shake my head, dismissing it. "I have to. If he really did this, I'll know. I need to know for sure. Whatever little bits of doubt are left in my mind, I need them erased. Dallas, he's my father—"

"Is he?"

"Don't play that game with me. If there's anyone who knows the import of blood ties versus legal ties, it's you and me."

He holds up his hands in defeat. "Jane, I—"

"I know. You want to protect me. We've been down that road before. Protect me all you want," I add with a magnanimous smile. "But just don't stop me."

8

Weight of the World

If I'd had any doubts that Deliverance was a secret organization, they would have faded by the time we reached the actual building.

Dallas took the most convoluted route possible. In taxis. On the subway. By foot. For all that trouble, I thought the place should be a palace. Especially since I've seen a Deliverance hub before, and that space probably rivaled the CIA in cutting edge tech and equipment.

But we're not standing in front of anything cutting edge. Instead, I'm staring at a ramshackle old grocery store in East Harlem.

I lift a brow as I look from the building to Dallas. "Seriously?"

But he just smiles and takes my hand as he leads me into the building. It's under renovation, and we move through the construction zone and into the small airspace between this and the next building. We enter that building through an emergency exit that opens into a stairwell, descend, then emerge in a small basement. The walls are concrete and smell of mildew. It's cloying, and I'm starting to get a little claustrophobic.

But then he strides past me and punches in a code on a hidden keypad. The doors creak open on mechanized metal hinges, releasing a hum of activity—the buzz of computers, the tap of keyboards, the low murmurs of voices. Dallas turns, holding out his hand for me. I walk the two steps to meet him, then put my hand in his.

"Welcome to the new Op Center," he says, and we step inside together.

The moment we cross the threshold, I see the change in him. Before, his focus had been solely on me, as if I were the thing that centered him. And while I don't feel abandoned or slighted, in this busy, bustling room, he seems to fill the space, growing even taller, more powerful, more focused. And considering Dallas has always had the air of command about him—even in his most playboy of personas—that's saying a lot.

I swivel my head, taking in the entire area—the banks of computers, the work desks, the dry-erase boards that cover entire walls and are filled with colorful notes and tacked up pictures. Two men I don't recognize sit in front of monitors, one talking on the phone, the other wearing headphones and bouncing slightly to some tune I can't hear while his fingers fly across a keyboard. I see Liam in the next room, separated from this one by a glass window. It appears to be a conference room, and he's speaking to someone who stands just out of sight.

The room is a mixture of tech and the almost clichéd feel of old detective movies. It smells of paper and sweat and stale fast food, and it's one-hundred-percent obvious that Dallas loves it here.

He's in his element, I think, and though I have always known that the kidnapping profoundly changed both of us, this is the first time that I truly see how far the ripples of that change have extended. This secret career that has been a driving force in his life. And though it started as a way to find our kidnappers, I know him well enough to realize it's now more than that. It's about us, but it's also about the others. It's about justice. And, yes, it's about the adrenaline rush of the chase. The danger. And the thrill of moments like this when he steps into a room in which every person is working toward that common goal of saving a life.

And then there is me. I've made a career out of writing about kidnappings, victims, and the like. Articles, books. Soon even a movie.

In other words, our trauma has become our art has become our passion. I don't know if that's good or bad, but I do know that it's our reality. And if there is one thing that I have learned, it's that you can't escape reality.

Dallas's posture shifts, and he cocks his head, his eyes narrowed in question. "Ready?"

"No," I say, but I move forward anyway, letting him lead me to where Liam has joined the two unfamiliar men, who stand as we approach, the red-haired man yanking off his headphones and tossing them onto the counter so that a faint drumbeat drifts up into the air.

"This is Noah," Dallas says, as I shake the hand of the man who'd extricated himself from the headphones. "And this is Anthony."

"Tony," the dark-haired man corrects, also offering a hand.

I don't have to ask if these men are good at what they do. Not only do their sharp, competent expressions telegraph as much, but I also know that Dallas wouldn't work with anyone who isn't at the top of their game.

"We're so glad you're okay," Noah says, then winces a little. "Well, that you weren't permanently hurt, I mean. So, you're here to talk about what you remember from the attack, right? Anything you can think of. We've gone door to door already, but the witnesses we've located haven't given us much.

"I'm still hoping to identify the van. We're still obtaining and analyzing footage from cams between the address and the dump site at Riverside Park," he adds to Dallas. "I'm not giving up yet, but so far we've got shit."

"Keep on it," Dallas says.

"Do you remember anything about the driver?" Tony asks me.

"No, I was—"

"Bro, she's here to talk to Colin, not slide into the hot seat. Not yet, anyway." The deep voice came from behind me, and I turn to see Liam. He holds out his arms. "So glad to see you up and about, baby girl. You gave us all a scare."

"Unintentional, I assure you," I say dryly. I've known Liam for almost my whole life, and along with Brody, he's one of my absolute best friends. His mom was our housekeeper growing up, so he's been around me and Dallas forever, and we three were an unbreakable trio up until the day Daddy sent Dallas off to London for boarding school.

Frowning, I glance around the room at these men. "It's not even dawn yet. Don't you guys ever sleep?"

Liam laughs. "In shifts, yeah. But when Dallas called, I got Noah and Tony out of the crib. I thought you would want to meet them."

"Definitely," I say, then smile at the guys. "Sorry to rouse you early."

"Part and parcel," Noah says. "Coffee's fresh and strong if you need it." He points toward a small kitchenette on the far side of the room, but I only shake my head. Coffee sounds a little too rough right now.

"Where's Quince?" Dallas asks.

"Just finished a session. Kept increasing the dosage throughout the night, still got nothing. Frankly, he's a little pissed with himself for pushing too hard. Now he's got Colin on a saline drip and some counteragents . . . working the drug out of his system." Liam glances at his watch. "Not too much longer, I'd think. We figured Jane would want to talk to him with as clear a head as possible."

"Good." Dallas turns to me. "He hasn't said a damn thing yet even with the drugs. You might be more effective than truth serum."

"Or I might not," I say. I don't add that maybe there is nothing for him to confess to. Dallas and the guys are already convinced. And, though I hate admitting it even to myself, their certainty has convinced me as well. Even so, I want to talk to Colin personally.

"Miss Jane." Across the room, Archie steps from the conference room, a smile wide on his face. I tug out of Liam's arms and run to him, then engulf him in a hug. He starts to pull away, but I hold on tight for another heartbeat, needing this connection to my childhood. A time when, as complicated as life was, things were simpler. A time when, though I now know that I'd been naive, I'd understood the people around me.

When I finally release him and step back, I find the Sykes family butler smiling down at me. "I cannot tell you how relieved I am that you're safe, Miss Jane. I won't say that all is well," he adds, his eyes softening, "because we both know that it isn't. But you are here and you are whole, and that is a very good beginning."

Despite everything, I smile. Yes, I'm standing in the middle of a criminal organization's safe house. Yes, *criminal.* Because even though an argument can be made that everything Deliverance did to rescue kidnap victims skirted against but never crossed any legal boundaries, there is no question that kidnapping Colin pushed them well into criminal territory, no matter how justified that action might be.

Dallas is at risk. So are Liam and Quince and all of the team, including Archie.

So, for that matter, am I. Accessory after the fact. I'd been married to an Assistant United States Attorney long enough to know that much at least.

And yet I'm here because even though I believe Dallas, I have to face Colin. With a sigh, I turn back to Dallas, my heart twisting a little when I see the expression on his face. Not just concern, but pity.

"I can handle it," I tell him for the umpteenth time. "More important, I can't move on until I hear it all from you guys, and then talk with him."

"I know."

I nod firmly, steeling myself. "All right," I say. "Tell me everything."

Liam and Dallas look at each other, and I can see the unspoken communication pass between them. Dallas nods, then takes my hand. "Conference room," he says. "We'll lay it all out for you."

And he does.

I sit numb in the leather chair as he and Liam flash documents up onto a screen, run through a timeline, and describe fact after fact after fact. They don't bother to speculate—they don't need to. The evidence is too damning. And each additional piece of information is like a stab through my heart.

Proof that Colin was in London at the time of the kidnapping—and that he'd used a false passport to enter the country.

A computer hard drive with damning emails between him and Silas Ortega, one of the six men who physically grabbed me and Dallas that horrible night seventeen years ago.

Proof that Colin wasn't in Boston as he'd told me when Ortega was murdered before he could cut a deal with the Feds. Instead, Colin flew to South America—which was where Ortega was being held.

Cryptic conversations picked up on a bug planted in Colin's

Brooklyn house. Conversations that suggested that Colin was in the process of liquidating his assets in order to disappear.

And on and on and on it went with dozens and dozens of little facts that at first just swam into my brain, but then connected together to form a picture.

I didn't know why he would do such a horrible thing to Dallas, much less to me, but by the time Dallas said, "That's it. That's everything we have so far." I was convinced. I might not know the why of it, but I was certain that Colin—my birth father—had been our Jailer.

"Are you okay?"

"I—" But I can't get the words out. Instead, a wave of nausea rises up inside of me, and I stand in sudden panic—and then vomit all over Dallas's shoes.

"Jane." He is on his feet immediately, pulling me close and holding me tight. Then he pushes back. "You shouldn't do this."

"No. No, I was just—thank you," I say as Liam hands me a glass of water. "It was just all too much. But I'm okay. Really." I wrinkle my nose and glance down. "Sorry."

He doesn't look convinced, but he kisses my head and slips off his shoes. "Come on," he says, then leads me to a bathroom complete with spare toothbrushes and toothpaste. I brush my teeth, then take the time to splash water on my face. Dallas has left, giving me privacy, and I lean forward, my hands on the counter as I peer into my own eyes.

"You can do this," I say, and I look so resolute that I almost believe it.

Then I step back into the main area to find Quince standing beside Dallas. The wall to my left is no longer solid. Instead, a section of concrete appears to have been removed, revealing what I assume is a one-way window. I can see Colin inside, seated at a table, his wrists cuffed to the tabletop.

I realize I'm biting my lower lip and force my attention back to Dallas. I draw in a breath, then kiss him hard. I need that connection. That reminder of what is good and right in my world.

And then I go with them to the door and wait as Quince punches in a code. Dallas stands by, his hands clenched into fists, clearly burning to go in with me. To protect me.

Suddenly, I don't want to step into that room. For hours, I've been thinking that I can handle this. That I'm strong. That I've been through so damn much that this is nothing—nothing at all by comparison.

But that's not true. My skin feels prickly. My stomach still burns. I'm alternately hot and cold, and at the moment there's nothing I want to do more than curl up into a ball and cry.

Except that's not true, either, because what I really want to do is run. Far and fast and away from this place and this man who so cavalierly hurt me. Hurt Dallas.

But I can't. I have to stay. I have to hear the truth from him.

Most important, I have to do this alone.

And so when the door slides open, I draw in a breath and walk on shaking legs into the cell to face the man who was once my father.

Now, I think, he is a monster.

9

Into the Breach

"Jane. Oh, thank god, Jane."

I hesitate just over the threshold, hoping that Colin can't see the way I'm shaking. I can still taste bile in my throat, and for a moment I'm afraid that I'm going to vomit all over again.

I don't turn around, but I know Dallas is behind me. I can practically feel the intensity of his eyes on my back, and I'm certain that if I show even the slightest sign of weakness he will come to my side, take my arm, and yank me out of this room.

Part of me wants him to do just that—to give me an excuse to turn around and not confront this man I once trusted.

But that's the cowardly part of me, and I don't want to be a coward. Not about this. Not anymore.

Right now, I need the truth as desperately as I need air and food and water. And so I straighten my posture, lift my chin, and walk across the room toward Colin.

Behind me, I hear the door click shut, and for just the briefest moment, I hesitate. Then I continue across the room, pull out a chair, and sit across from my birth father.

I fold my hands in front of me so that I'm sitting much like he is. Except that my wrists aren't attached to the table with iron. My fingers are twined together, and I'm clenching them more tightly than is comfortable. I hope I look casual. As if this whole experience isn't killing me. As if I don't feel like I am trapped in a nightmare.

"Jane," he says.

"Why?" I say at exactly the same time.

Colin shakes his head. His eyes gleam as harsh lights reflect off his tears. "No," he says. "No, baby, you have to believe me. What they say I did—I swear to you. I didn't."

His words squeeze my heart, and I wish I could believe. But I've heard too much.

I push away from the table and stand up. Then I turn my back on him and head toward the door, my heart pounding so loud I'm sure he can hear it.

As my hand closes over the knob, his cry of "Jane!" stops me. I hesitate, and then I turn. I say nothing, though. Just look at him expectantly.

"Don't go. Please, please don't go."

I shift back toward the door. "I'm not interested in lies, Colin. I came for answers. If you're not going to give them to me, then I'm just wasting my time." I grasp the knob again, and this time I turn it. I give it a tug, and it swings open a fraction of an inch.

"I didn't want to! Oh, god, Jane, I made a mistake. The most horrible mistake!"

His words slice through my heart, and I squeeze my eyes closed. *I will not cry. I will not cry.*

What I want to do is race from this room and into Dallas's arms. What I do instead is close the door, slowly turn around, and walk back to the table. I keep my eyes on the ground, though. I'm not prepared to look at him. Not yet, anyway.

Once I'm seated, I blink and swallow as I take a mental inventory. I don't want him to see on my face how much his sideways confession has hurt me. I don't want this man to see me cry. "All right." I lift my head. "Tell me."

"Ortega approached me," he begins.

"How did you know him?"

"I didn't. I'd never met the man. But I'd heard of him. Through, well, some of my other business connections."

I raise my brows at the word "business," but say nothing.

"He—well, he was connected. Intimidating. He—he had his fingers in a lot of things. We overlapped on the smuggling, and he got my name somehow. Said I was on his radar. I don't know why. He didn't say." He raises his hand as if he is going to reach for his face, but the motion is aborted by the cuff and chain that keep him attached to the table. Irritation flashes in his eyes, and I get the impression that he's lost his stride.

I wait.

Colin fidgets, then continues. "He said that he'd been watching me, and that led him to watching Eli. And Eli's bank account. He said that he learned about what your mother did, and Eli. About how they took you away from me." His voice cracks with emotion. "I was wrecked then—I tried not to show it to you, but losing you just about destroyed me. I was hurt. Angry. Everything. I lost my way, sweetheart." A fat tear spills from his eye. "Totally lost my way. And then Ortega said he'd had his eye on Eli as a mark—that he wanted to snatch Dallas and hold him for ransom. I was horrified—I was!—but then Ortega said that he wanted my help. That taking Dallas would be a way to punish Eli. To punish Lisa. To twist the knife in them the way they'd twisted it in me."

I'm fighting not to cry—I can't believe that he would even think about doing that, much less go through with it.

"I was angry. Hurt. I wanted to get back at her. At Eli. I

wanted to punish them, and I shouldn't have. Oh, god, I shouldn't have." He dropped his head into his hands, his shoulders shaking as he sobbed.

"How did you help?" My words are hard. Cold.

Slowly, he raises his head. "I—I told him where Dallas went to school. I answered questions when he planned and hired the men. But that was all. I swear, that was all. And I needed the money—you remember how bad off I was—I needed the money and he said that just for that information I'd get half."

"They—they took me, too." I hate the way my voice cracks. I don't want to show emotion. I don't want him to see just how much he hurt me.

"I know." His tears come in earnest now, and he has to bend his head down almost to the table to wipe them. There is a box of tissues on the far side of the room, but I don't get up to bring them to him. "He told me afterward, and I flew into a rage. You weren't supposed to have been there, and I begged him to let you go. But he said it was a perk. More money. And when I told him he could have my share of Dallas's ransom if he just set you free, he laughed and told me I was a fool. Jane, Jane, sweetheart, you have to know I would never do that to you."

But I don't know that. I don't know anything anymore.

"Were you there? In the cell with us?"

"No! No, I went to London because Ortega told me I had to. He told me how to do it so that nobody would know. But I just stayed in a flat he'd rented for me."

"And the Woman?"

"Who?"

I hug myself, suddenly cold. "There was a woman. She—she was vile."

"No." He shakes his head, his brow furrowed. "No, the whole team was made up of men. There wasn't—"

"Bullshit," I say as I push my chair back and stand. I yank out my phone and pull up the picture of me on the ground. I

shove the picture in front of him, then point to my face, where the bruises still linger. "*She* did that to me. And she did worse—so much worse—when we were teens."

He's shaking his head. "No, no. There was no woman. There wasn't."

I turn around and head for the door.

"Jane, wait! Don't leave. Please don't leave me."

I round on him in sudden fury. "Then tell me the truth, goddammit. For once in your life just tell me the fucking truth!"

"I am! I swear! How can you believe I would do this? I don't understand what's happening. I don't know why you won't believe me. I've told you I was involved. I was an idiot—it was stupid and horrible and you're right to hate me. But, sweetheart, there's nothing left to tell."

"There was a woman," I insist. "Tell me about her or I walk out that door."

"Yes, yes, okay, yes, there was a woman. She was Ortega's girlfriend, and I know she brought your food, but I barely knew her. She's dead now. She's been dead for over a decade."

"Bullshit."

"It's true. It's true." Tears track a path down his face. "Jane, sweetheart, please. I love you. I love Dallas."

A wild fury rises inside me, culminating in the explosion of a single word—"*Don't.*" I draw in a breath, forcing myself back to some level of calm. "Don't say that. And don't you dare say his name again. You gave up that privilege seventeen years ago."

"What are they going to do to me? What are you going to let them do to me?"

"I don't know," I say, then deliberately turn my back on him and step toward the door. "Honestly, I really don't care."

10

Restraint

"Don't do it, man."

Dallas took his eyes off Jane long enough to glance sideways at Liam. "What are you talking about?"

"Don't put your fist through the glass. It's a bitch to replace."

Dallas's mouth quirked in an ironic smile. "I'll keep that in mind," he said as Jane paused in front of the door, listening as Colin said he loved her. That he loved Dallas.

Fucker.

"She did well." Quince leaned against the wall at the edge of the window.

"You believe him?" Liam asked, the incredulity clear in his voice.

"Not a word," Quince said, then immediately corrected himself. "Well, one or two words. He did go to London, and he definitely knew Ortega. He may even genuinely love you and Jane," he added, with an eye toward Dallas. "At least in his own twisted way. But the rest of it? Utter fabrication."

"Can you get him to admit it?"

Quince lifted a shoulder. "Yesterday, I would have said absolutely. Today, I say probably."

"Why? I thought he was susceptible to the drugs."

"He is. Possibly a little too susceptible. The standard dose completely narced him up. Cross a line, and all you get is nonsense. Truth, fantasy, remembered bits of bad television shows. He talks, sure, but it's like he's dictating a wild dream after a long night of drinking tequila. Can't put much stock in that, mate."

Dallas nodded. "All right. So you play with the dose. More time, but eventually you get there."

"That's the plan," Quince said. "And as for the bit about the Woman being dead, I'm going to hook him up to a polygraph, but I need to wait at least forty-eight hours for the drugs to fully clear his system. If he's the lying asshole we think he is, that supports the theory that Jane's attacker was the Woman. If he's telling the truth, well, that's something we'll have to factor in."

"Do it as soon as you can," Dallas said, as they watched Jane turn back to the door, pull it open, and step outside to join the men.

Dallas was at her side even before the door clicked closed behind her.

She looked up at him, her expression hard. Visibly, she was keeping it together. But he could see the cracks. Her red-rimmed eyes. The tension in her jaw and shoulders. With the notable exception of his ruined shoes, she'd handled everything that had been thrown at her with remarkable aplomb.

But even a woman as incredible as Jane couldn't keep absorbing the blows. And he was afraid that if she kept taking hits, she was going to shatter.

"He says it wasn't his idea," she said. "He says the Woman is dead."

The words seemed to stab him through the heart. "I know. I heard. Do you believe him?"

Her throat moved as she swallowed and tears spilled from her eyes, cutting tracks through her makeup. "Not a goddamn word." She gasped a little, and then, as if the words broke through a dam, her tears came in earnest. He pulled her close, holding her against him as sobs racked her body. His arms were tight around her, and all he wanted in that moment was to take the pain from her. To make her forget. To help her cope. To erase the horrible truth that was cutting through her. Destroying her.

But no, that wasn't really all he wanted to do. What he wanted more was to burst through that door, put his hands around Colin's neck, and squeeze until he'd snuffed out every bit of life remaining in the man. A man who claimed to love him, to love Jane. A man who hurt them. Who lied to them. Who'd run roughshod over their lives, destroyed their childhoods, and left both him and Jane broken.

Broken.

No matter how much he wished it wasn't, he knew damn well it was true. They coped—and god knew they coped better together than apart—but that didn't change the simple fact that Colin's fucked-up kidnapping scheme and what happened inside that cell had broken both of them.

There was no going back; they could only move forward. And Dallas knew that killing Colin now couldn't change the past.

But it would feel so damn good.

He closed his eyes and pulled the woman he loved closer. If it weren't for Jane, he doubted he'd even try to rein himself in. But because he knew it would wound her even more, he battled back the urge. Nothing was more important than Jane. Protecting her. Loving her.

Even if that meant letting a worm like Colin live.

After a moment, she pushed gently away from him, her head

down. He hooked a finger under her chin and tilted her head up. "I'm so sorry."

Her thin smile just about broke his heart. "I've known the truth for days now. But it's different hearing it—or *not* hearing it." She hugged herself, her shoulders rising and falling as she sighed so heavily he felt her breath on his face. "I guess I thought he'd be honest with me."

"Would that matter?"

"Maybe. No. I don't know." She sighed. "I didn't even cross-examine him." Her shoulder lifted in a shrug, as if she wasn't sure where she was or what she was doing. "I know everything you told me. Where he's been. When he traveled. I could have demanded explanations. But I just couldn't stand to hear his bullshit."

"Oh, baby. It's okay. What do you need now? Mom?" If she said yes, he'd find a way, no matter how much it pissed off their father. "Brody?" he asked, thinking that as much as it might sting, maybe she needed her best friend. Someone not in their fucked-up family. He twisted slightly, searching for Liam who had quietly slipped away the moment Dallas had taken her in his arms. Maybe she'd want him, their friend who'd stood like a rock with the two of them throughout childhood, but wasn't a man she was in love with.

But then she said, "Just you," and he thought his heart was going to melt.

He lifted her hand to his lips and gently kissed her palm. "Home," he said. "I'm taking you home."

"I'm sorry," he said once they were in a taxi and on their way.

She tilted her head. "For what?"

"What he did to us. That he didn't own up to it today."

The corner of her mouth rose ironically. "That's hardly something you need to apologize for. And honestly, I don't think it matters what he said today. It doesn't really change anything, does it? Whether he tells us the truth or not, there's still some psycho bitch after us."

Pressing her fingertips to her brow, she shook her head. "Oh, hell. Now I'm the one who's sorry. It's just that . . ." She stopped herself, then sighed. "I was just thinking about, well, everything. And sometimes I wonder if I should have kept quiet that day the press saw us kiss. Maybe we should have let them believe that bullshit story you made up about it being a dare. Because that was the beginning, Dallas. That's when the psycho bitch came out of the woodwork. Whether she's the Woman or some crazed female you got naked with, that very public kiss and my very public statement are what set her off."

He didn't argue. How could he when she was right?

"And it's not just her," Jane added. She glanced toward the Plexiglas barrier between them and the driver, then turned back to Dallas, apparently satisfied that the driver either couldn't hear or wasn't interested.

"That kiss brought the press swarming in," she continued. "I mean, let's face it. I wasn't that interesting before. And while you've been a regular on Page Six for ages, the news that you're fucking your sister pretty much kicked your social media stock into overdrive. How much do you want to bet they'll be waiting for us when we get home?"

"I'm going to pass on that bet. I'm not flush enough lately to risk losing."

As he hoped, she smiled. "Yeah, my bank account's a little thin these days, too." She sighed, then shook her head as if exasperated with herself. "I'm just frustrated. I want a life together—a real life. And I'm starting to wonder how the hell we're ever going to make that happen."

"But we will," he promised, though he had no idea how. He slid close to her and put his arm around her shoulders. She curled against him, and he sighed, relishing the way they fit perfectly together. "Somehow, we're going to make it happen."

She tilted her head up to his. "Do you really believe that?"

"I do," he said, then bent to kiss her. Immediately, she opened to him, and in that moment he truly felt as if he really was the one thing she needed in all the universe, and if they could just figure out a way to make the rest of the world go away, then everything would be all right.

"I want you now," she murmured, trailing her fingertip back and forth over his thigh and making him just a little crazy. "I need you inside me. Please, Dallas. I want to feel you next to me, and then I want to fall asleep in your arms and sleep away the whole rest of the day."

"The whole day?" he teased. "It's barely nine in the morning."

"Then you'll just have to tire me out, because I'm done. When I wake up, I want it to be tomorrow."

He slid his hand along her inner thigh, then felt his cock twitch at the sharp sound of her breath as she gasped with anticipation.

He pulled his hand away, and watched her eyes narrow. "Any more, and I won't be able to stop."

"I don't want you to stop. Not ever."

"You do want me to stop," he said as he gently brushed his thumb over her lower lip. "Because we're almost home. And we both know the vultures are going to surround us the minute this car pulls up in front of the building."

For a moment, he thought she was going to protest that she didn't care.

For a moment, he almost wished that she would.

Then the spell broke and she nodded once, then slid out of his embrace and over to the far side of the bench seat. For a second, he fantasized about pulling her back and kissing her so hard they'd trend all the way to the number one spot on Twitter.

But that was only a fantasy.

He'd find a way, though. Somehow, he was going to find a way to be with Jane. Truly and completely and openly.

And on that day, he'd tell the damn reporters to all go to hell.

Today, he just kept his head down as they emerged from the taxi. As he'd predicted, the second the vehicle had pulled up, the reporters and paparazzi who'd been casually leaning up against trees and parked cars rushed forward, so many of them that Dallas swore some must have emerged from the sewers like rats.

"Jane! Dallas!" Their names echoed in the crisp morning air, underscored by the honk of taxi horns, the squeal of brakes, and the general din that was Manhattan during rush hour.

"Dallas! What are you going to do now that you're no longer the CEO of Sykes Retail?"

"Jane! Are you still speaking with your parents? What about Colin West? Was your birth father aware of your relationship with your brother?"

"Are you going to stay in New York?"

"Is it true that Lyle Tarpin turned down the lead in *The Price of Ransom*? Is it true that the studio has pulled the plug on the movie altogether?"

Beside him, Jane winced. Dallas frowned; that was a new rumor, and one he could tell from her expression that Jane hadn't heard. He hooked an arm around her, lowered his head, and dove into the throng, resolved to get them both through the gauntlet without any more bombs landing squarely on top of them. By the time they reached Howard, the doorman who'd come out to meet them, his arms held wide in an effort to shield them, Dallas was in a foul mood.

"They've been loitering all morning," Howard said. "I'm

sorry, Mr. Sykes, so long as they stayed in the street and away from the entrance there was nothing I could do."

"You were great," Dallas assured him. "And I'm sorry about it. I imagine we're the most unpopular people in the building right now."

Howard immediately assured him otherwise, but the expression on the older man's face suggested that Dallas was one-hundred-percent right. *Damn celebrity chasers.*

He kept his head down and Jane tight against him as Howard ushered them the rest of the way into the building, and he kept her close as he guided them onto the elevator and then punched the number for their floor.

Only when the doors closed and the car was moving did he relax his hold on her. He turned to see her face, expecting her expression to be guarded, his own anger and frustration in her eyes.

But when she lifted her head, all he saw was need, and he had only an instant to process that reality before she flew into his arms so violently that he stumbled backward against the elevator's glass wall.

The intensity of her kiss burned through him like wildfire, and he pulled her tight against him, his mouth claiming hers, one hand cupping her rear as the fingers of his other hand wound tight in her hair so that he could have her where he wanted her. But what really got him hard was the knowledge that this was exactly where she wanted to be, too. In his arms, finishing what they'd started, erasing the whole goddamn world, if only for a little while.

"Please." The pure passion of her voice rocked him, and when her hand cupped his crotch, he thought he would explode right then. But when she started to tug down the zipper of his jeans, he caught her wrist in his hand.

She tilted her head back to look at him, her lips swollen, her face flushed.

"Cameras," he said, hating that they had to be so damned rational, because god knew he'd been sucked off in elevators before. But he couldn't risk security cam footage of him and Jane suddenly showing up on Gawker.

For a moment, he regretted his words, afraid that the reminder of the eyes that were constantly on them would push her back into herself. But then she smiled, slow and sexy, before pressing her body hard against his, her pelvis tight against his cock, as she whispered, "Then you damn well better strip me naked the second we're inside the apartment."

He was fighting the urge to do exactly that despite the damn cameras when the elevator stopped and the doors slid open—and there was Bill Martin, standing right outside the door.

"Finally," Jane said in that same moment, her back still to the door. "I need you to fu—"

He pressed a finger to her lips even as he plastered on a false smile. "Hello, Bill," he said, and watched Jane's eyes go wide as she spun around to face her ex-husband. "You want to tell me what the hell you're doing here?"

Dallas eased his arm around Jane's waist and led her into the hall. "For that matter, how did you get in here?"

Bill opened his wallet and flashed his badge. "It's not as impressive as when I worked at the US Attorneys office, but it's official."

"WORR's not the FBI," Dallas said, referring to the World Organization for Rescue and Rehabilitation. "It doesn't have investigative power in the United States." He kept his words tight. Focused. He couldn't show fear, only irritation. Bill had to be here because he wanted to investigate the Sykes kidnapping against the family's specific request that he back off. This wasn't about Deliverance. It wasn't about Colin.

At least he hoped to hell it wasn't.

Bill shrugged. "All I did was show your doorman the badge.

He didn't ask questions, just let me up. Talk to him if you have a problem."

"My problem is with you," Dallas said. "Now get the fuck away from our front door."

"I need to talk to you." He turned to Jane. "To you both."

"Not a good time, counselor. Now I'm going to ask you politely again, and then I'm going to get testy. You don't want to see me when I'm testy, so I suggest you get out of my way. She needs to sit down."

"Where the hell have you been? It's the crack of dawn, Dallas. You two decide to just pop out to watch the sunrise? Grab a really fresh bagel?"

"Bill, please." Jane's voice was so thin that Dallas could barely hear it. Bill did, though. That much was obvious by the way his combative expression faded to sympathy.

"Oh, shit. Jane, I'm sorry." He stepped aside, and Dallas inserted his key in the lock, then held the door open for Jane. "Wait," Bill called. "Please. I talked to Lisa. She told me about the attack. That's the only reason I showed the badge. I just needed—I just needed to know she was okay. *You* were okay," he added when Jane turned to look at him.

"I—" she began, but Dallas cut her off.

"Go inside, baby. Let me talk to Bill for a second." When she hesitated, he cupped the back of her head and pressed a kiss to her forehead. "Sweetheart, please. I'll be right behind you."

He hated seeing the fear that flooded her eyes, and Dallas wished that he could reassure her. But they both knew the stakes. Knew who Bill was and what he might figure out. Right then, though, Dallas had to gamble that Bill was still clueless about Deliverance.

For a moment, he thought she was going to argue, but she acquiesced, and with one final glance toward Bill, she went inside.

Bill took a step, as if he intended to follow, and Dallas neatly parried. "Not happening."

"Dallas, I just—"

"What? Want to see her? You saw her. Christ, Bill, she was attacked and beaten and dumped at the curb like garbage. She's hanging on by a thread." She was doing a hell of a lot better than that, but Jane's emotional state was no longer Bill's business.

Bill's eyes dipped down to Dallas's crotch. "Is that what she was hanging on to?"

"Do not go there," Dallas said. "You think this is a joke? All for the publicity? This is our life, hers and mine, and you have fucked with it royally."

"Now, wait a minute. I—"

"*No.* You wait a minute. What the hell were you doing, telling her that the FBI and WORR were looking to arrest Colin for my kidnapping? And then telling her that he's disappeared? Did you think that would be easy on her? Did you think that she could just deal with it, because what's one more thing piled on top of all the rest?"

He was playing a dangerous game, and he knew it. As far as bad ideas went, pissing off the man who was trying both to prosecute your kidnapping without your consent and track you down because, unbeknownst to him, you happened to have abducted his prime suspect . . . well, that was just wrong in about a dozen different ways. But somehow, Dallas couldn't make himself shut up. His emotions were so damn pent up after days of holding them in, that now that the surface had cracked, everything was spewing out. Even things against his better judgment.

"You know what, Sykes," Bill countered, real irritation flashing across his face as he stepped closer to Dallas. "I'll own that—sure. I made it harder on her. I guess I thought she needed to know the truth about what was going on. But you still haven't answered my question. If she's so fragile, where the hell have you two been? You just decide to go for an early morning stroll?"

Fuck.

"Where we go and what we do isn't any business of yours anymore, Bill," Dallas said, as calmly as he could manage.

"I guess not," Bill said coldly. "I'm just her ex-husband. You're her brother. It's not like I could legally marry her. Sleep with her without risking a felony charge. Oh, wait," he said, cocking his head like he'd just remembered something. "I *could* do all that. You're the one who can't ever really have her."

Ice shot through Dallas's veins, and the only reason—the *only* reason—Bill wasn't facedown, unconscious on the floor that very second was that Jane was mere feet away behind that door, and she'd dealt with enough already.

From his sharp intake of breath and the quick step backward, it was clear that Bill knew he was lucky to be standing.

"I think you need to leave now, Bill."

"Shit, Dallas," Bill said, his entire body seeming to deflate. "I just want a few minutes."

"Bill," Dallas repeated, "it's time for you to leave."

11

Lost in You

As soon as I'm inside the apartment, I close the door behind me and force myself not to shake. Bill shouldn't scare me—he shouldn't. I know the man. Once upon a time, I even loved him, or at least I thought I did.

But now not only is he hurt, he's certain he's got the moral high ground on his side. And I'm afraid that Dallas is so intent on taunting the man who used to sleep with me that he's going to make some verbal misstep and somehow reveal to Bill his role in all of this.

What will Bill do when he finds out that Dallas is behind Deliverance? That Dallas and his team are interrogating Colin in an East Harlem cell?

I cringe, realizing that my concern isn't *if* Bill will make that discovery, but *when.*

Oh, god, I hate this. I truly hate it.

And right now, I want to move, but to where? I want to act, but how? It's all well and good for Dallas and me to say that we will carve out a life together in the world, but we still have to attack that fundamental question of how exactly that's going to happen.

Unfortunately, I'm pretty sure that taunting Bill isn't getting us closer to that goal.

Frustrated, I move away from the door, my entire body feeling like lead pushing through pudding. I'm exhausted, both mentally and physically. Apparently being unconscious for more than twenty-four hours doesn't count as quality sleep. Couple that with the fact that I've been up all night, and I guess my bone-deep weariness makes sense.

I don't want to sleep, though. I want Dallas, and I'm heading for the kitchen to grab a cup of coffee when my phone rings. Liam gave it back to me as Dallas and I left Deliverance, and the sound, so unfamiliar after a few days without it, makes me jump.

I fumble inside the small purse I've been carrying with me, then frown when I see the caller is Joel, who is producing the adaptation of my book, *The Price of Ransom,* for film. I consider ignoring it, but then take the plunge and answer. At the moment, dealing with Hollywood is probably a hell of a lot easier than dealing with reality.

"Joel?"

"Janie, sweetheart, where the fuck have you been? I've left messages? I've sent emails? What? You fall off the planet or something?"

"Or something," I admit as I set the phone on speaker and put a cup under the Keurig. I glance again at the time. "Why are you calling so early?" It's three hours earlier in LA, and I know from experience that Joel rarely rolls into the office before ten.

"What? I can't touch base with my favorite writer?" He chuckles, as if that is the cleverest thing ever said. Then he clears his throat. "Seriously, Janie, the new pages are brilliant, absolutely brilliant. I only have a few notes."

"Great." I don't actually mean that. I've learned that in Hollywood, everything is said in code and double-talk, and a "few notes" probably means a massive rewrite.

"And Lyle may have a few issues, too."

I'd been reaching for my freshly brewed coffee, but now I pull my hand back as slowly as if a snake were coiled in front of me. "Issues?" I repeat, remembering what one of the reporters had shouted about Lyle turning down the lead. Which, considering Lyle is rising fast in Hollywood and is already one of the most bankable stars, would be disastrous.

"I thought he loved the book," I continue. "And the script. Your last email said that he was completely in love with everything I've turned in."

"Baby, baby, baby. He does love it."

"Then what are we talking about?"

"You just let me handle this. Lyle's a sweetheart. He adores you."

"But?"

"But you need to leave this to me."

"You're not making me feel better." I drag my fingers through my hair. "Should I call him? We've talked. I thought we clicked. Maybe it could help?"

"I'm on it, Janie. I'll figure a way to turn this shit around. We'll use it, if we have to."

"Use it? Use what?"

"I won't let this deal go south. Don't you worry your pretty little head."

I ignore his condescension. "Joel, are you saying—" I draw in a breath. "This is about me, isn't it? He's pulling out because of me and Dallas." Never in a million years would I have dreamed that the gossip about me and Dallas hitting the press would mess up my movie deal.

"I'm not saying a damn thing, sweetheart. And you're not worrying. You write notorious books. You've got a notorious reputation. Baby, we are all over that shit."

Notorious.

We ended the call but when Dallas walks in a minute later, I'm still mulling over that word—and the situation.

Can it be true? Could the media bullshit surrounding Dallas and me really destroy my most lucrative and high-profile deal?

And how the hell had I not even considered that this might happen?

"Jane? What's wrong?"

I actually laugh, because how am I supposed to pick the best answer to that question? Bill, work, Colin. Honestly, the list is pretty much endless.

I settle on just shaking my head. "Joel called. Just bullshit with the screenplay."

Dallas studies me, but says nothing. Instead, he takes my hands and pulls me close. I sigh deeply and snuggle against him, wanting to just get lost here in his arms. "Baby, you're dead on your feet."

I tilt my head back and offer a weak smile. "I am," I admit, then rise up on to my tiptoes to brush a kiss over his lips. Because though I'm tired, sleep isn't what I want or need. "Please, Dallas. Bring me back to life."

"I can do that," he says, then releases me as he takes a step backward. "Take off your clothes."

The shift from gentle to commanding surprises me, but also excites me, and the no-nonsense authority in his voice makes my pulse pick up tempo.

"Jane." His voice is stern. "Now."

I feel the impact of his words between my thighs. A wild heat builds inside me, and I'm eager to simply surrender and let Dallas take charge. I'm wearing jeans and a silk tank top under a Prada blazer. I take the jacket off first, and toss it carelessly aside. My arms are bare now, and the air against my skin is almost as erotic as the way Dallas is now looking at me.

"Jeans next," he says, and I comply, slowly unbuttoning the fly and then wriggling my hips to slide off the denim. I'm wearing a thong, and I take it down with the jeans. Since I kicked off my flats as I entered the apartment, my feet are bare, and I step out of my clothes and take a step toward Dallas.

I'm half-naked now, wearing only my tank and satin bra. I lick my lips as I take one more step in his direction.

"Stop," he demands. "Now spread your legs and close your eyes."

I do as he says, feeling vulnerable, exposed, and wildly turned on.

For a moment, there is silence. I hear only my own breath and the faint hum of the air conditioner. I imagine him watching me. My nipples erect under the thin tank. My pussy wet and throbbing for him. I'm already desperate for him, and he hasn't even touched me.

I wait as long as I can stand, and when he still says nothing— when the urge to slide my fingers between my legs and satisfy this building ache becomes overwhelming—I whisper, "Dallas?"

"Shhh," he says, his voice coming from behind me. I feel him take the hem of my tank, and I lift my arms as he pulls it over my head, then tosses it aside.

"Dallas . . ."

"No talking," he says as he frees me from my bra. "No moving. No anything. Not unless I tell you to do it."

"Okay," I murmur, then jump when his palm lands hard on my ass, the sweet sting so surprising and arousing that tremors of electricity shoot through my body to gather at my core, a precursor to a full-on orgasm that will surely bring me to my knees.

"Did I ask you to answer?"

I almost respond aloud just so that he'll spank me again, but instead I shake my head.

"Good girl," he says, his voice coming from in front of me. "Now spread your legs. That's it," he says when I comply, and I hear his soft, slow intake of breath before he says roughly, "Christ, that's hot. Your nipples hard. Your areolae dark, just waiting to be sucked. And your pussy—baby, I like that you wax for me. Do you want me to touch you? Do you want me to slide my hand over your cunt and feel how wet and slick you are?"

"Yes." I can barely get the word out, I'm so turned on.

"But I am touching you," he says, and now his voice is soft. He's moved silently toward me and is whispering into my ear, the soft caress of his breath like a kiss. "My hands are cupping your breasts and my thumbs are teasing over your nipples. They're so hard, and I flick them lightly with my finger-nails."

I startle as he says that, and I swear I actually feel his touch. I open my mouth to cry out his name, but then remember the rules and press my lips together.

He chuckles. "So obedient," he says, and as he speaks, he strokes a soft finger from my core to my clit, and I tremble, my pussy clenching in a futile effort to draw him in, to have him fill me.

"Your reward for being so good," he says. "Do you want me to touch you there more?"

"Yes," I beg shamelessly. "Please, Dallas. Please."

"I am. Don't you feel me? The way my fingers play with your clit? The way I'm standing right in front of you, the cotton of my shirt brushing your sensitive nipples as my hand cups your mound. I'm sliding my palm over you, baby, and you're so wet, and it feels so good, and you're holding on to my shoulders because your knees are so weak you can't stand up on your own."

I say nothing; I can't remember if he's asked me a question.

"Answer me, Jane."

"I feel you," I say, and I do. I can imagine his touch, the light strokes, the heated tease. The way he plays me so perfectly because he knows me so well.

"I'm on my knees now, baby, and my hands are on your hips. Tilt forward for me," he demands, then says, "That's it," when I comply.

"Can you feel my tongue?" he continues. "How I'm stroking you, teasing you? And oh, baby, you taste so good."

It's incredible, but I can feel it. Not only that, but my body is reacting to it. That telltale tightening in my thighs. The way my skin prickles, as if I've gone outside in a lightning storm. That's Dallas, a storm upon my senses. And I can't help but think that any man who can take me this close to orgasm without even touching me definitely deserves his reputation as the King of Fuck.

"I want you to come for me, Jane," he says, and though I want to—though I'm so wildly, wonderfully turned on—I'm not sure I can cross that line.

"Now," he orders, and as soon as the word is out of his mouth, I feel the soft brush of his breath between my legs, teasing my clit, mimicking his touch. I imagine that he's leaning in, ready to put his tongue on me, to close his mouth over me.

I imagine that . . . and I explode.

As I do, my legs really do go weak, and the world seems to spin out from under me. I keep my eyes closed because he hasn't told me to open them, but I can feel the world falling away from me.

And then I'm caught, captured in a bridal-style carry in his arms, and his lips are on mine, and he's murmuring to me. Telling me I'm exceptional, I'm beautiful, I'm the most amazing woman he has ever known.

"And you're mine," he says. "How fucking incredible is that?"

His words make me smile, and I snuggle against him. I'm completely sated, and I feel thoroughly fucked, and it's weird, but at the same time it's not because this is Dallas, and he has always had a magical effect on me.

He takes me to the couch and I curl up against him as he pulls a blanket over us. "What about you?" I murmur, barely able to keep my eyes open.

"Believe me, baby, I'm just as satisfied as you are." He brushes my hair off my face and kisses my forehead, and I close my eyes again as he uses the remote on the coffee table to turn on the stereo. It's a classical station and so soothing, and I close my eyes and simply drift, happy to have released the burdens of the day, even if for just a little while.

I don't know how long I stay like that, my head resting on his shoulder, my naked body pressed tight against him, with only a light blanket over me. I feel remarkably well taken care of, like something precious to him. *Something fragile,* a small voice in my head adds, and I can't help but frown.

"Tell me what you're thinking," Dallas says, because he never misses a trick.

I consider lying, but since I almost left him over secrets, that would be wildly hypocritical. So I tell him, and he just shakes his head.

"You're far from fragile," he says. "If you were, you couldn't have put yourself back together all those years ago."

"Have I? I mean, I spent my adult life in various self-defense classes and it didn't do me a damn bit of good when that bitch tased me."

"Anyone can be a victim to a determined attacker."

He's right—I know he's right—but I still feel argumentative. Probably because when I think about the attack I still feel scared. Vulnerable. And that's not a feeling I like.

Purposefully, I shift the conversation. "You haven't told me about what happened out in the hall with Bill."

"Not much to tell," he says. "He's worried about you, jealous of me. And," he adds with a hard edge to his voice, "he seems suspicious about where we were at the crack of dawn."

Immediately, I stiffen. "Do you think he suspects something? About you? About Deliverance?"

"I don't know." He shifts, rolling over a bit so that we're face-to-face. "But I will say that he's the last person I want to talk about while we're naked."

"Oh, really?" I start to trail a finger down his chest. "So what do you want to talk about? Or do you want to talk at all?" I ask as I follow the arrow of hair down his lower abs to his cock.

I see the heat flare in his eyes and bite my lip in anticipation of round two. He reaches down, and though I expect a sensual touch, he surprises me by closing his hand over mine.

"I want to know what put that look in your eye when I came into the apartment. What did Joel tell you? Are our shenanigans wreaking havoc with the financing?"

I grin at the word "*shenanigans*," but have to nod. "Joel says he'll handle it. Apparently Lyle has some issues. Apparently they're with us."

"You met him, right?"

I nod. "Yeah. We got along great."

"So talk to him now. This movie is important to you?"

"You know it is."

"Then go after it. Don't wait for Joel to work it out. You want Tarpin, go after him."

I consider that. "I am good at going after men that I want," I say in a teasing voice. "I went after you and got you, didn't I?"

He chuckles, and I feel the vibration rumble through me.

"Yeah, well you already had me. I was just in denial. So were you, for that matter."

"Until I decided I couldn't live without you."

"Well, go to Los Angeles and do the same with Tarpin. Except," he adds with a wry grin, "not exactly the same."

"You'll come with me?"

"Baby," he says, flipping me over so that I'm on my back and caged between his arms. "I'm always with you."

12

Sunshine on My Shoulders

I haven't owned it long—only since I sold the film rights to my book and started to write the screenplay—but my LA home is one of my favorite places. It's situated just off Mulholland Drive, and I love the way the back of the house is mostly glass with a view of the hills and the city below.

It's always full of light, and the yellow walls and the bright photographs that I've hung in the bedroom make it so cheerful, that I inevitably smile whenever I wake up here, and today is no exception. Especially since Dallas is here with me.

Except he's not actually here.

We'd managed to catch the last flight out last night, and had arrived at the house at just before midnight California time, which is three in the morning in New York. We'd gone straight to bed and I'd fallen asleep in his arms. I'd expected to wake up that way, and now I look toward the bathroom, but there's no sign of him there, either.

The bedroom door is ajar, however, and I hear the soft murmur of words. I frown, wondering who's in the apartment, then I realize he's on the phone.

"I haven't heard from him, either," Dallas says. "I know. I'm worried, too."

There's a pause, and then he says, "You know Colin, Mom. He probably took off with some buddy and is in the middle of the Caribbean on a yacht trying to close some sort of deal."

I wince. Because, of course, Colin is about as far away from a sun-soaked yacht as you can possibly get.

He ends the call before I get out of bed, and by the time I'm done in the bathroom he's finishing another call. "All right, sounds good," he's saying as I walk into the room. Then he slips his phone in his pocket and smiles at me. "Good morning, beautiful."

"Good morning, yourself," I say, sliding into his arms. He's already showered and dressed in jeans and a pale green T-shirt that brings out his eyes. He smells like soap, and I breathe deep. "I heard you talking to Mom."

His smile downshifts to a frown. "She's still trying to get in touch with Colin. She's starting to get worried."

"Yeah, she would."

"Adele's concerned, too," he continued. "She called about ten minutes before Mom did."

Immediately, I tense.

"Jane," he says tenderly. "There's nothing—"

"I know." I snap the words at him, though the truth is I'm mostly annoyed at myself. I step back out of his arms under the pretense of getting coffee; I feel silly about my reaction, and don't want him to notice how tense Adele's name makes me.

"Was that who was just on the phone?" I ask casually as I head toward the kitchen.

He follows me, and from the hint of a grin on his mouth I'm

certain he recognizes my tactic. "No, that was Damien. I've got a meeting with him tomorrow."

"Damien Stark?" I've started to fill the coffee carafe, and now I look up. Stark is a former professional tennis player turned billionaire entrepreneur and the CEO of a business conglomerate that makes our Sykes family business look like a garage sale. Dallas and Damien have worked together before, but that was because Stark Real Estate is developing some projects with Sykes Retail. But since our father fired Dallas after he learned about our relationship, that project is no longer Dallas's concern. "What's the meeting for?" I ask. "You're not with Sykes Retail anymore, so . . ."

"Not Sykes business," he says. "Tech stuff for Deliverance."

My eyes go wide.

"Damien doesn't know about Deliverance, though he may suspect something. Don't worry," he says in response to my look of shock. "I trust him."

"All right," I say, still a little nervous. "So what's the tech?"

"Noah designed a listening device. It's groundbreaking. Allows you to essentially have ears on an entire building from a single operational point. It has the potential to be huge in the market—and exceptionally useful for an entity like Deliverance."

I nod; I can see that.

"Since I can't manufacture it without garnering attention, we licensed it to Stark. He builds it, pays Noah a royalty, and sells the tech back to me at a highly discounted rate."

"I get it," I say. "And so the meeting's about that?"

"Exactly."

"But that's tomorrow. You don't have any work planned for today?"

"Not a thing. You?"

The coffee has started brewing, and there's enough in the

pot for a half cup each. "Not a thing," I say as I grab two mugs and pour us each a shot of caffeine. "Joel's in Palm Springs today on a set, but he's got Tarpin coming in tomorrow afternoon, so I guess I have a chance at keeping him on the picture." I gulp my coffee. "So this works out great. We're both free, and today we're going to do nothing but have fun."

"Is that a fact?"

"Not just a fact, it's a plan." I kiss him, then back away with a grin. "Give me ten minutes to get changed, and the fun will begin."

He chuckles and I hurry to my closet to find something to wear. When I return, I'm in a sundress and flip-flops. He looks up, his expression of concentration shifting to appreciation as he watches me do a little twirl, making the skirt flare.

"What are you working on?" I ask, heading toward him.

He puts the tablet down and shakes his head. "Nothing we need to worry about today. Where are we going?"

"I was thinking Universal Studios." I love that theme park. The rides are great, but what I love the most is the tram that takes you around the back lot so that you can see old movie and television sets. "And after that, maybe hit a bar near the beach and have a drink on the patio."

"Lead the way."

As it turns out, the day goes pretty much as planned. We spend about three hours at the theme park, eating fast food and holding hands on the rides and strolling through the movie memorabilia shops.

After that, we rejoin the throng on the CityWalk outside the park entrance and browse the various shops that line the retail area. We buy matching Hollywood ball caps and put them on. Mostly just because we're being silly, but they have the added benefit of making us less recognizable.

Not that that's much of an issue. I've seen a few people do a double take when they look our way, but I've decided to attribute that to the fact that Dallas is so incredibly gorgeous, and not to any notoriety the two of us might have.

The only change in the plan is that we don't go to the beach. Universal is in Studio City, which is just over the hill from my house, and neither of us want to deal with LA traffic to get to the coast. Instead, we pop into Gelson's and buy grapes, pâté, cheese, and crackers, along with champagne and caviar.

Back at the house, we take the food and some wine out to the back porch, saving the caviar and champagne for the evening.

We spend the rest of the afternoon curled up together on the giant round lounge chair I'd bought when I'd purchased the house. We snack and drink wine and read and talk. And we touch and kiss and snuggle. It's more intimate than sexual, and I absolutely love it.

On the whole, the day is perfect. But by the time evening rolls around, I'm ready for something more. Something hotter.

Something like Dallas. Naked.

Naked and inside me, actually.

He shifts on the lounge chair to refill his wine and grins at me. "I can read your thoughts."

"Can't."

"No?" He trails a finger from my collarbone over my breast and all the way down to my clit.

I whimper. "Well, maybe you are a little psychic."

He kisses me gently, but though I expect it to build to more, he pulls back and asks me, "Are you worried about tomorrow?"

I think about it. "Not really. Even if I do lose the movie, I'll still have the book. I talked to my agent, and she says she's not concerned on that front at all. *Code Name: Deliverance* is moving forward."

"Is it?"

I make a face. "Yeah, well, I may end up changing my theme

a bit." The premise of the book is the damage done by vigilante groups. And while I still hold to that theory where some groups are concerned, I've changed my mind about Deliverance now that I know who the players are and I've seen it from the inside.

"If Bill ends up arresting me, you can turn it into a memoir."

I shoot him a hard look. "Don't even say that. I can't— Dallas, if something happened to you . . ."

He pulls me closer. "I know. God, baby, I know."

I hear the catch in his throat, and it suddenly hits me just how well he does know. Because something *did* happen to me.

"I'm so sorry you had to go through that," I say.

"Me? Oh, baby . . ." He cups my face, and I see something flicker in his eyes. "I want—"

"What?"

"You."

My smile blooms bright. "You have me."

"I want more. I want—" He stands, and I frown at him, not sure what's going on. "I want us. I want everything."

"So do I. But we both know that everything is impossible for us. We're going to have to settle for what we can get."

"I'm not the kind of man who settles, Jane. You know that."

I do, but I can't imagine where he's going with this. I've done the research, and no state in America allows adopted siblings to marry. And most states—including our home state of New York—consider our sexual relationship to be criminal incest.

For that matter, I couldn't find any *countries* that would allow us to be together. I found a vague reference on the Internet that suggested that adopted siblings could marry in Sweden, but I haven't been able to confirm it.

And, honestly? I don't want to move to Scandinavia.

"Dad's going to be at Stark's office tomorrow," he says. "I'm going to talk to him about rescinding my adoption."

My eyes go wide. "Can you do that?"

"I've been doing research. It's not common, but there is precedent. But Dad will have to be on board."

"Dallas, I don't think he'll—"

He presses a fingertip to my mouth. "Don't say it. Tonight, just believe it will happen. Okay?"

I nod. "It's just that—"

But this time he silences me with a kiss, and when he closes his mouth over mine I forget what I was even going to say, and just lose myself in this man I love.

13

Stars Shine Down

Dallas let himself drown in the heat of her perfect mouth that he had loved forever, that was more essential than oxygen to him.

She opened to him eagerly, as if she could never have enough of him, no matter how deep the kiss, how violent the connection. He understood. He craved her with an intensity like nothing he'd ever known, and though he couldn't remember a moment when he hadn't felt that way about her, the blinding, tunnel-vision-like need for her had only increased over time, until now she was an addiction. Hell, she was blood, oxygen, a goddamned life force.

Jane was everything. She filled his days and sweetened his nights. She lightened his heart and satisfied his soul.

And the way she sucked his cock was one hell of a mark in the plus column.

He chuckled at the thought, and she broke their kiss, her brow lifted. "Something you want to share with the class there, mister?"

"Kissing you just made me think about all the things you can do with that mouth of yours."

She didn't answer, but he caught the mischievous gleam that fired in her eyes before she shifted her position on the lounge chair so that she could kneel beside him. Then she lifted the hem of her tiny little dress just enough to hook her fingers under the band of her panties and tug them down to her knees before she shifted again and pulled them all the way off.

Aiming a sultry smile his way, she let them dangle from her fingertip before she tossed them aside.

"All right," he said. "You have my attention."

Her laughter bubbled through him, filling him with pleasure. It seemed as though it had been forever since he'd heard such spontaneous joy from her.

"You just reminded me of all the amazing things that *you* can do with *your* mouth."

"Is that right?" he said.

"Mmm." It wasn't much of an answer, but if he hadn't already understood what she had in mind, he would have figured it out when she swung her leg over his waist and straddled him so that her back was facing him. "I'm pretty fond of your fingers, too. Just saying."

She bent forward so that she could lower his fly, lifting her ass as she did so that he had one hell of an enticing view of the back of her dress clinging to the curve of her rear. He reached forward, cupping her ass cheeks and then slowly lifting the skirt to reveal the smooth white skin of her ass and the sweet, wet flower of her cunt.

"Christ, Jane," he said, arching up in wild pleasure as she eased his cock from his jeans, then took the head into her mouth. He thrust his hips up, wanting her to take him deeper, wanting to feel his cock slam against the back of her throat even as his fingers slid deep, deep into all her secret places.

"That's it, baby," he said as she wiggled in response to the two fingers he slid inside her. "Suck my cock while I fuck you. Deeper, baby," he demanded, thrusting his fingers inside her as she obeyed and sucked him so hard it was a wonder he didn't explode right then.

But no, not yet, and he forced the explosion back, his whole body tense with the effort to halt this erotic assault on his senses. The feel of her mouth on his cock. The sight of her cunt and her ass, open and ready for him. The scent of her arousal, sweet and sensual. He was primed to explode, but he couldn't. Not yet. Not until he'd taken her to the edge. And certainly not until he settled her sex on his mouth and sucked her clit with at least as much passion as she was sucking his cock.

First, though, he wanted to tease her. He wanted her dripping. He wanted the slightest brush against her clit to send her spiraling. He wanted her crazed.

He wanted her to lose herself to him.

Slowly, he teased her core with the tip of his thumb, then stroked her sensitive perineum. She rocked her hips, silently begging for more, and spread her thighs wider, opening herself to him even more. He doubted she even knew what she was doing, positioning herself to be taken by him while she sucked him. Exposing herself like this. Intentionally making herself so goddamn vulnerable that it brought him to his knees knowing how open she was to him, how much she trusted him.

He wanted to give her every kind of pleasure he could, and he gently pressed his sex-slick finger against her ass, edging along the rim, urging her to relax and open to him. With his other hand he reached around her, then found her clit and stroked. Gently at first, and then faster as she bucked and moaned, and he slid his finger in deeper and deeper.

Every time she shuddered in pleasure, the assault on his cock changed, interrupting the steady, building pressure, and leaving him frustrated and on edge until finally he couldn't take it any longer and he pulled his hands free, grabbed her hips, and moved her toward him so that her pussy was on his mouth and he was tasting her sweet juices and, holy fuck, he could not get enough of her.

And he sucked and licked as she ground against his mouth, her lips still teasing his cock as his own hips moved in a wild, steady rhythm, as if he was the one in charge—the one fucking her mouth—instead of vice versa. Because at the moment, he was totally and completely under her spell.

His entire body was tense, sensitive. As if his body was too big for his skin and he needed to break free. And dammit, Jane was the only one who could take him there. And her mouth was working a magic on his cock that he was trying to duplicate. A steady rhythm. A pattern. And damned if it wasn't a pattern that led him right over the edge, because her mouth was magic, and she was sucking him, the wet sounds of her lips on his cock filling his head, making him even harder.

So hard that he was going to explode—and he forced it back, wanting to feel her rock against his face, her own release in time with his. He pulled her closer, sucking hard as he did, taking all of the frenzy that was ripping through him and putting it back to her, kissing and sucking and teasing until he could feel the vibrations of her moans of pleasure against the tip of his cock, and that was it. That was what tossed him over.

"*Jane*," he cried as he exploded, his orgasm rocking through him even as Jane shattered above him, her mouth still on his cock, as she sucked him dry.

When they could both breathe normally again, he pulled her up to him, and they stretched out together on the lounge beneath stars.

"I love you," she said.

"Oh, baby. I know." Gently, he stroked her pink cheeks and swollen lips and thought she was the most beautiful creature he'd ever seen. She was his, dammit, and Dallas was willing to move the world to make that simple reality a stone-cold fact.

Unfortunately, in order to move the world, he first had to move his father.

14

All Knotted Up

The next morning, Dallas stood in the reception area of Damien Stark's penthouse office. He'd arrived early, and he was using the extra time to catch up with Liam as to the progress with Colin.

"It's slow going," Liam said. "Drugs aren't working on him. But Quince is good at what he does, and he'll get what we need. It's just not going to be fast, or easy."

"Fine. Well, no, it's not fine," he corrected himself, "but it is what it is." He shifted so that his back was even more to the petite receptionist, then lowered his voice. "How the fuck did I miss the signs? How did I look straight at that man for so many years and not see who or what he was?"

"You saw what he showed you," Liam said. "You saw what he wanted. Hell, I did, too."

"He's had training," Dallas said. "It takes a certain skill set to withstand Quince's interrogation. And still I never picked up on it."

"There were a lot of years when he was off your radar," Liam pointed out.

"And a lot when he wasn't."

"Don't beat yourself up about it. The man's good. Hell, he's a fucking chameleon. We saw what he showed us. Not the monster underneath. That's the thing about monsters, Dallas. They don't just hide under children's beds and in dark closets. They hide right in front of us. That's what makes them so damn scary."

Dallas ended the call when the receptionist called his name to get his attention. He turned and found her standing. "They're ready for you."

He nodded, then took a deep breath as he started down the hall behind her. Time to go see a different kind of monster.

"What the hell are you doing here?" Eli Sykes demanded, staring at his son who was striding into the conference room.

Dallas stood a little taller, the motion designed to hide his disappointment. He hadn't actually expected a warm welcome from his father, but some small part of him had been holding on to hope.

He should have known better.

"I have a meeting today with Damien. He mentioned that you were coming to the office this morning to go over the San Diego and Culver City retail sites. I asked if I could have a few minutes." He glanced at Damien, who was rising from his chair across from Eli. "I appreciate you letting me intercede on your time."

"Well I don't," Eli said. "Damien, your schedule may be flexible, but I assure you mine isn't. I have no time to spare for foolishness, sentimentality or, god forbid, begging."

"I understand completely," Damien said as he walked to the door. "As it happens, I've had an emergency come up that's going to keep me away for the next twenty minutes. You're welcome to spend that time however you see fit. As is Dallas." He nodded between the two of them. "I'll see you both later."

When the door closed behind him, Dallas took the seat that Damien had just vacated. "I have a proposition I want to put on the table."

"This is absurd," Eli said, pushing back and starting to rise.

"*Listen to me.*" Dallas's words sliced like a hot knife through the tension between them, and for a moment, Eli froze and father and son simply stared at each other.

Then the spell seemed to break, and Eli shook himself and rose to his full height, his brow furrowed and his eyes blazing. "Listen to you?" he repeated. "Listen? To what? To you telling the world that you're sleeping with your sister? That you've made a mockery of our family? Is that what I'm supposed to listen to, Dallas?"

A thousand retorts filled Dallas's head, but none seemed sufficient to counter his father's vitriol, and he stood there, numb against the pain of his father's verbal lashing.

"You just couldn't keep it in your goddamn pants. Maybe I can understand when you were children—the trauma, the fear—but to continue this, this *farce*. To intentionally embarrass this family by behaving that way with your sister. Your *sister*. Well, I cannot—"

"Then don't."

The words came out so hard, so hot, that Eli actually shut his mouth and took a step backward.

"You can't stand the fact that Jane and I are siblings? Then fix it. *End* it."

Eli's jaw tightened and his face turned a deep purple. "What the hell are you talking about?"

"Rescind my adoption."

"What?"

"Make it go away," Dallas pressed.

"You're talking nonsense." Eli shook his head slowly, as if

Dallas wasn't making a bit of sense. But he was. Just like he'd told Jane, he was certain this was the way. Hell, it was the only way.

"It's not nonsense," he continued, trying to keep his voice calm. Rational. His dad was a businessman after all, so Dallas needed to approach this as if it were a deal. An offer on the table for a move that might be risky, but in the end could make all their stock go up. "We'd need to file a petition in the same court that entered the adoption order, and we'd both need to consent along with Mom, but if—"

"And pile on even more embarrassment? Make us even more of a laughingstock? Drag this family even deeper through the mud than you already have?"

With each word, Dallas felt his temper flare even as he seemed to sink farther and farther into himself.

"Absolutely not," Eli said finally. "Out of the question."

"Dammit, Dad, this isn't about public relations. It's about your children. About our lives. Let us be free to love each other."

"I've already answered that question."

"You're punishing me—punishing us—because we fell in love."

Eli cocked his head and looked straight at Dallas, nailing him with the no-nonsense glare he used so often in the board-room. "No, son. I'm punishing you because you acted on it."

15

The Hills Have Eyes

I'm driving to the studio where Joel keeps his production office when Dallas calls to tell me that all did not go well with our father. And though I can't help but be disappointed, I am not surprised. Rescinding the adoption would be the perfect solution for us, but for Eli Sykes, it would be admitting he'd made a bad decision.

And while my father is more than willing to change course when it comes to business, he's not so swift to own up to mistakes where his personal life is concerned.

I tell Dallas as much, and he reluctantly agrees, though there's no denying the disappointment that colors his voice.

I'm disappointed, too, of course, but I think I'm less surprised. I know Dallas believed that faced with the choice of being selfish or helping his children, Eli would come out on our side. But it's only been a day since I walked into my birth father's cell. A man who did the most heinous thing possible to his child, and for purely selfish reasons. So nothing much shocks me anymore.

"Do you want me to cancel my meeting? I can go back home and we can do whatever it takes to make you feel better. *Whatever* it takes," I repeat, purposefully injecting a lascivious tone into my voice.

As I'd hoped, he laughs. "That sounds wonderful, but you need to see Joel. Besides, one of us needs to have a meeting today that doesn't go south."

"Does that mean things with Damien went badly, too?"

"No, no. Everything is fine on that front. In fact we're thinking about flying out to Riverside to look at the actual production facility. They have a working prototype that I'm anxious to see. But that will put me home late. I hate to miss our dinner."

"Don't be silly." He'd suggested we go out tonight, but it's not as though the LA restaurants are going away any time soon. "We can have the champagne and caviar on the back patio, then maybe watch a romantic movie, and then who knows where the night will lead . . ."

"I like that plan," he says. "I'll call when I'm getting close. Your day is going okay?"

"So far, it's perfect. Don't jinx me."

"Wouldn't dream of it," he says. "I love you," he says, and I'm amazed at how much depth and emotion can fill three little words.

I'm still smiling when I hand the security guard my ID and he lifts the gate to let me onto the lot. Joel's office is in the back, behind a section of false-front houses that represent a neighborhood I've seen on some television sitcom, but damned if I can remember which one.

I park, square my shoulders, and head inside.

Despite Dallas's prediction that my meeting will go better than his, I'm not holding my breath. On the contrary, I'm prepared for Joel to be overly conciliatory and Lyle to be full of excuses. I don't expect either one of them to actually call me a pariah, but I'm certain that's what they'll both be thinking.

And I'll have to smile and nod and pretend like I'm doing just great despite the fact that this amazing career opportunity is crashing down around my ears because the press has decided to get all up in my personal life.

That's what I anticipate, and I'm even ready for it, so I march into Joel's office with my back straight and my loins girded, whatever the hell that means. Bottom line, I'm ready to take the punches and roll with them.

But the blows never come. On the contrary, we really do talk about the script, just like Joel had promised. Both men are friendly and businesslike. I take notes, we discuss changes, argue about character motivation, and ponder combining or cutting a few scenes to make the overall story flow better.

In other words, there's nothing personal or unprofessional at all—and I get no indication that Lyle is pulling out of the project.

I'm relieved, and also a little baffled. So baffled, in fact, that when Joel checks his watch and says that we have to wrap because he has a dinner meeting in Santa Monica, I blurt out, "But what about—"

I cut myself off, realizing that perhaps it's not the best strategy to remind Lyle he was supposedly pulling out.

For a moment, Joel actually looks blank. Then his eyes dart quickly to Lyle before he shakes his head and says, "Sweetheart, it's all good. You just go write. We got this shit covered."

"Oh." I'm surprised, but pleased. Mostly, I'm hoping this means that my stock on social media has fallen.

Lyle walks me out to my car. "I'm guessing Joel told you I might pull out of the picture?"

I glance sideways at him. "He might have mentioned something along those lines."

Lyle laughs. "Yeah, well, I just want you to know it wasn't me. My publicist got all in my face about it, but I told her to drop it. I love the script, and I think this project has a lot of potential. I'm in it for the long haul."

"Wow," I say. "Thank you for telling me. That really does make me feel better."

He shrugs, and for a moment I see the quiet Iowa boy the papers all say he was before his family moved to Hollywood when he was sixteen. "I thought you should know. Especially since Joel apparently would rather pretend none of the controversy even exists," he adds with a wry smile. "And I also want to say that I'm sorry your personal life is being plastered everywhere. I know how hard that can be. I chose to live in the spotlight but you didn't, and it sucks that you have to deal with it."

"I really appreciate that," I say, meaning every word. "It's been hard, but we're getting through it."

We chat politely for a few more minutes, and by the time I get to my car, I'm actually smiling. I have yet to be accosted by rabid reporters, my colleagues are understanding, and I'm still glowing from last night under the stars with Dallas. Our dad may not be on board with our plan, but that's okay. Today, I'm swimming in optimism.

I decide to hit the gym before grabbing the food, and not only is my trainer actually free, but we get in a kick-ass workout that leaves me feeling completely recharged. I may not be able to deflect Tasers like the one that took me down in New York, but just knowing that I've got a seriously mean kick makes me that much more self-confident.

We still have caviar and champagne in the house, but I pop into Whole Foods to get some brie, and although a few people do a double take when they see me, I'm hardly big news today. Apparently Garreth Todd, Hollywood A-lister and a fan favorite, was spotted in the produce section. The girl who checks me out tries to act like this is old hat, but I can't help but notice the way she keeps twisting around, as if hoping to catch a glimpse as he moves through the aisles.

Even my house is paparazzi free, and I can only guess that's because no one knows I'm in town. My neighbors are far enough away that they may not have noticed when the taxi dropped us off yesterday, and since I keep my car in the garage and the lights are on a timer, from the outside the house looks the same whether I'm living in it or not.

And, of course, even if the neighbors do know I'm here, it's not like they're going to call TMZ. All that would do is clog their street and front yards, too.

Which means Dallas and I may actually have privacy for a few more days.

I like to think this means the universe is rooting for us.

Dallas texts me that he's about to board Stark's helicopter to return from Riverside to downtown LA. He has a rental car at Stark Tower, so he promises to text me again once he's about ten minutes away.

No problem, I text back. *But I'll be starving. Guess that means you miss out on my pre-champagne sexy dance.*

If I beg?

Try it, I tell him. *I do love it when you're on your knees.*

Since I'm alone, I open a bottle of wine, then kick back and watch two episodes of reality TV—the kind of stuff Dallas knows I watch, but I absolutely won't admit to. I also shower and wash my hair, change into a short skirt and sheer blouse, and take extra care with my makeup. When I'm dressed and feeling girly and sexy, I head to the kitchen to pull out my best dishes and crystal.

I've just put the champagne in a bucket of ice when Dallas calls. "I'm at the bottom of the hill. I should be there in ten minutes. If you're naked, I can think of some very intriguing ways to enjoy caviar."

I laugh. "I'll take it under advisement. And I should warn

you—I've already had a glass of wine. Sort of an appetizer for the champagne," I say, and he laughs.

"Apparently, I have some catching up to do."

"Definitely."

I refill my glass and then pour one for him. Then take them both out with me to the front porch. And then, when I see his headlights at the far end of the street, I leave his glass on the railing and step off the porch to meet him.

At first, I don't even notice the dark lump in the middle of my driveway. When I do, my first reaction is irritation that one of my neighbors left their trash so unsecured that a trash bag blew over onto my property.

But then Dallas turns into the driveway.

His headlights illuminate the lump.

I see tangled flesh.

I see blood.

And then, of course, I scream.

16

Too Many Maybes

Dallas was out of the car within seconds, pulling Jane into his embrace and blocking her view of the poor, brutalized dog that someone had viciously murdered and left in the driveway. "You're okay. You're okay."

"Someone d-did that. I saw its throat. Someone did that and brought it here. For us." She tilted her head back, looking at him, her eyes so large and scared that Dallas was certain he would have put his fist right through the heart of whoever did this. Whoever hurt that poor animal. Whoever scared Jane.

"I know, baby. I know. Let's get you inside."

She let him lead her toward the patio, her body frail against his, as if this new assault had knocked the foundation out from under her, and if she wasn't careful she would tumble and shatter.

No.

No way was he letting that happen. She was too strong, and she'd already survived so much. She'd get past this. They both would.

They'd survive.

They'd do more than survive.

And they'd make whoever did this pay.

"The Woman did this," Jane said. "She attacked me in New York, and now she's taunting me here."

"Maybe." Dallas raked his fingers through his hair. "Probably. But I didn't expect her reach to be quite this long. We didn't exactly make it public knowledge that we were coming to LA."

She said nothing as he pushed the front door open for her. She shook her head. "No. I want to stay with you."

"I need to call the cops and wait out here for them. I don't want anyone tampering with the scene."

"Who—"

"I don't know. Maybe no one. But there are coyotes in these hills, too, and buzzards. I need to stay out here."

"Then I'm staying with you."

"Jane, I don't know. You—"

"Can handle it," she said firmly. "I'm scared, sure. Because honestly, I'd be an idiot not to be. But this is my house, and that bitch came onto my property. So I'm pissed, too. And pissed trumps scared."

He studied her and saw the fight under the fear, and for just a moment he felt like an ass for even trying to coddle her. She was a survivor. He should know; he was a survivor, too.

"All right," he said, then dialed 911.

To the department's credit, two officers arrived within ten minutes, and Dallas joined them when they examined the dog. For that, Jane opted to wait on the porch. Dallas half-considered doing the same—someone had used barbed wire to strangle the poor collie—but he didn't trust the police to not overlook something important. As it was, both Dallas and the officers zeroed in on the collar and dog-tag.

The older cop—Sergeant Fielding—held it out while his partner took a picture of the owner information, and Dallas used the opportunity to memorize the name and phone number. *Carol Lucas.*

"Know her?" Fielding asked.

"Not that I recall," Dallas said. "But the name's vaguely familiar. I know a lot of women," he added, and saw Fielding's partner smirk. "Give me a second," he added as he pulled out his phone.

"Do you know the owner?" Jane walked over to join them. At the same time, two cars pulled up and parked on the opposite side of the road. The drivers' windows came down, and cameras started flashing.

"Dammit," Dallas said, pulling Jane with him as he turned around and hurried back to the house. "Tabloid chasers. They must listen to the police band. Come on." He urged her inside the house, and then stood just inside with the door half-open so that they could hear the police outside, urging the men to move along.

Dallas was barely paying attention to that, though. Instead, he was following a trail from Carol Lucas's Facebook account and then to her Twitter and Instagram profiles. He remembered her vaguely—a pretty blonde he'd slept with twice when he'd been in Los Angeles a year or so ago. He'd blocked her on Twitter after their second date when she developed the annoying habit of sending him tweets every five minutes on the nose.

Now he saw what he'd been missing. A tirade about what an asshole player he was. How he fucked her and dumped her. How he deserved to have his heart yanked out and stomped on. Those started about eight months ago, and the general theme had continued periodically until recently.

But in the last few weeks, she'd started posting about him and Jane. Words like *"perverted"* and *"sick fuck"* and *"skanky bitch"* showed up with alarming regularity.

He'd never thought she was violent. Never even gotten a hint of a vibe.

He damn sure had a vibe now.

But was that because Carol Lucas was the real sick fuck? Or because somebody wanted him to think so?

"Do you really think it's her?" Jane asked later, once the officers and the crime scene unit had cleared the scene.

"Honestly? No." He'd told the police everything he could remember about Lucas, and they promised to keep him in the loop. He had no intention of waiting for them to report back, though, and he'd already texted Liam with the relevant details and instructions to dig into Lucas.

"Me neither," Jane said. "She's too young to be the Woman. And even though my stalker might be some deranged former fuck of yours, I don't really think so."

"We also have to factor in that the attack on you in New York was planned. That van was ready to whisk you away. Unless Lucas is bi-coastal—and I don't think she is—that would be a hard job for her to coordinate."

Jane nodded. "Which means the Woman is using Lucas's crazy tweets as camouflage."

"Exactly." They were inside on the sofa, the bottle of wine on the coffee table in front of them, and the caviar and champagne forgotten. He topped off Jane's glass and handed it to her. She took a gulp instead of a sip, the only outward sign that she was still shaken.

"That means she followed us to LA," Jane said. She shuddered, then took a smaller drink of wine. "That means she's watching us. Always watching us. That completely freaks me out."

"I know."

His phone buzzed, and he glanced at it. An incoming call from Adele. He switched it to silent.

"You should answer it," Jane said. "Those reporters. She probably caught our act on the Internet and is calling to make sure we're okay. For that matter, I should call Mom, too."

He wasn't in the mood for Adele, but he also knew Jane was right. So while she took her phone into the kitchen to call their mother, he answered Adele right before the call rolled to voice-mail.

"Are you both okay?" was the first thing she said. The second was, "Between you and Colin, my hair's going to turn completely gray before the week is out."

"We're fine," Dallas said. "Shaken up, but fine. But what's going on with Colin?" He kept the words casual. Surely she didn't suspect that he'd been snatched. They'd deal with it if some sort of official investigation had begun surrounding Colin's disappearance, but it was much neater if the world simply presumed that he was off on a jaunt, as a man of some wealth and a spurious background might be inclined to do.

"What's going on is I still haven't heard from him. I'm starting to get worried, Dallas. It isn't like him to stay out of touch for so long."

"Have you been to his house? Anything look out of place?"

"I went two days ago before I headed out of town myself. All locked up nice and tight, but of course I have the key. His passport's not in his safe—"

"You have access to his safe?"

"Well, not officially, but we were married for years, and he never did bother to change passcodes. I used the old combination, and it worked."

"But that's the answer, then. He went overseas on a whim. He's probably in Aruba soaking up the sun."

She made a disbelieving noise.

"Fine," he said placatingly. "I'll be back in a day or so. We'll go to his house, check his calendar, his financial records. We'll make a plan, and if he hasn't turned up by the weekend, we'll go to the authorities."

"You don't think I should call the police now?"

"I think it would be premature, but if it would make you feel better . . ." He said the latter because it seemed like the reasonable thing to say, but he kept his fingers crossed in the hopes that she wouldn't take the suggestion.

After a moment, she sighed. "Perhaps you're right. I'll see you soon?"

"I'll call you when we get back."

"And Jane is doing well? The horror of that poor animal after her own attack—she may look like she's coping, darling, but you need to keep an eye on her. That girl has been through a lot."

"I know. You're right. And we appreciate the concern, but I promise I'm taking good care of her."

Her laughter was like the trill of bells, and actually made him smile. "Yes, I imagine you are. Well good night, pet. Kiss kiss." She clicked off before he could say goodbye, and he tossed his phone on the table, then reached for his wine, realizing that just talking to Adele had been an emotional workout.

"She okay?" Jane asked, returning from the kitchen.

"Worried about us and Colin. But she's fine."

Jane's frown was mostly hidden behind her wineglass as she took another sip, her hand shaking just enough to make the wine slosh.

"Hey," he said, taking the glass and setting it on the table. "What are you thinking?"

"Everything. Today. Just all of it." She shifted on the couch when he held out his hand for her, then scooted over to settle between his legs, her back to his chest. "I want to cry for that poor dog."

He wrapped his arms around her and pressed his lips to her hair. "I know." He tightened his grip, unconsciously pulling her closer, keeping her safe against him.

"This day started out so perfect. I kept expecting Joel or Lyle to say something stupid. Or someone to recognize and harass me. But nothing. The day was so smooth. So easy. And I want to kick myself now because I feel like I let my guard down. Like *we* let our guards down."

"Maybe we did a little, but I don't think either one of us would have expected this."

"No, I don't think so, either. But, Dallas, we shouldn't have to keep our guards up all the time. I don't want to live like that. No, I *can't* live like that. Feeling like we can never relax. Never just be ourselves."

"Oh, baby." He wanted to tell her she was wrong, but how could he argue with what she was saying when she was so plainly right? They were trapped, lodged in on one side by a psychopath and on the other by the reality of their own relationship. A relationship that by its nature kept them both in the spotlight and subject to constant criticism and comment.

"He has to tell us." Her words were barely a whisper, so low Dallas wasn't entirely sure he'd heard her right. "Somehow, we have to make him tell us."

His chest tightened. She hadn't once asked about Quince's progress with Colin since they'd left for LA. He closed his eyes, measuring his words, then said slowly, "There are ways. More extreme methods that Quince hasn't turned to yet."

A shiver ripped through her, so intense he felt the ripples in his own body. "Whatever the ways are, you have to use them. Because I think she's been watching you all along—on and off for the last seventeen years."

What she was saying wasn't a revelation. "And now she's gone off the rails because we're back together." It wasn't a question. He knew that was where she was going with this train of thought.

"Exactly. She thought she'd broken you back then. Thought that you were her little toy that she'd played with and put away in the closet. Maybe she didn't like the way you had all those women, but she could handle it. It was detached. A distraction."

"But you're not," he finished. "And she can't stand that."

"Exactly." She sighed. "That's why we need to talk to him. We need to let him know we don't believe his bullshit that she's dead. And honestly, even if *he* believes it, he still needs to tell us what he knows. Maybe she faked her death. Maybe she let him believe she was gone. But he knows something, and we need to find out what."

She twisted in his arms to look at him. "What?" she asked when she saw that he was smiling.

"I just love you."

Some of the tension faded from her face. "I love you, too. And that's why I'm tired of waiting for the other shoe to drop. Before, it was being discovered. Now, it's maybe being killed. I want to own my life. You're the only one I'm willing to let have power over me. Not this bitch. Not ever again."

"Agreed. I'll tell Quince to push harder."

He watched her throat move as she swallowed, then pushed herself up so that she was sitting, her legs over his on the couch. She took his hand. "And we need to tell Mom."

"She already knows we suspect it's the Woman."

"No. I mean we need to tell her about Colin."

"Baby . . ."

"She deserves to know."

She was right, of course. He hated it, but she was right. "And you need to ask Bill why he thinks Colin is guilty," he added.

"Dallas, no. I don't want—"

"Depending on what WORR has on him, we can use it in the interrogation room. But more than that, it's too suspicious if you don't ask. Of course you'd want to know."

"Right. Of course you're right." With a sigh, she closed her eyes.

Gently, he squeezed her hand. "Hey, are you okay?"

A single nod, then a deep breath. Then she opened her eyes and looked at him. "Yes. No. I don't know. I guess I still feel like we're in that cell, and she's watching us. Shining some big spotlight on us. And just like rats in a maze, she's waiting to see how we're going to get out. What our next move is."

And though Dallas didn't say so out loud, he knew exactly what she meant. And he hoped to hell their next move was the right one.

17

Shards

"She ruined our evening, you know." I'm standing in the kitchen looking at the bucket of champagne and thinking about the caviar chilling in the fridge. "Fucking bitch."

Dallas is still in the living room, and he comes toward me with the now-empty bottle of wine. "If the evening is the only thing she takes from us, I'll consider that a victory."

I take the bottle from him and slam it down in the recycler so hard it breaks.

"No," I say, "that's not victory. I want to be rid of her. We need to be rid of her." My phone rings, and my first instinct is to just toss it into a drawer and slam it shut. But then I see that it's Brody.

"Call him back later," Dallas says, but I shake my head. Then I take a breath to calm down and answer the call.

"How's my favorite New York exile?" Brody asks as soon as I pick up.

"Not having the best day, actually."

"Oh, shit." His tone immediately changes. "Did something

else happen? Do you have any news about who attacked you? You and Dallas aren't—"

"We're fine," I say, reaching for Dallas and giving his hand a squeeze. "We're about the only thing that is."

"Oh, kiddo, I'm sorry. Bad news about the bitch who put you in the hospital?"

"No news," I say. "But more drama."

"Fuck," he says, his voice heavy with concern. "Something else happened. What?"

"Honestly, I don't want to talk about it. I'll tell you when I see you next. In the meantime, if you go on social media, I'm sure it'll be trending by morning."

"Fuck, fuck, fuck, I'm so sorry you have to deal with this shit."

"It's definitely not fun. But like I said, I'm shaking it off. Or trying to anyway." I actually shake my arms and head, as if sloughing off the bad shit. "So," I say brightly, "did you just call to check on me?"

"Actually, my timing sucks, but I called for a favor. I was wondering if I could maybe use Dallas's bungalow for the week. Get there tomorrow afternoon sometime?"

Dallas is an investor in The Resort at Cortez, an island vacation destination off the coast of Los Angeles operated by Stark Real Estate Development. And, as an investor, he owns a private bungalow in a gated section.

"Sure. I mean, I should check and make sure he hasn't promised it to anyone, but I don't think there will be a problem. Hang on."

I ask Dallas, and of course he says it's fine, which I relay back to Brody.

"That's great. Thank you, and thank Dallas for me."

"No problem. But what's the occasion? Just looking for a getaway?"

"Pretty much. I just—I just want to surprise Stacey."

I frown, something in his tone worrying me. "Is she okay?"

He chuckles. "I'm not allowed to surprise my wife?"

"I know you, remember? Your idea of a surprise is to rent a romantic comedy instead of an action flick."

He barks out a laugh. "I don't think I'm that uninventive, but I take your point. And yes, everything's fine. Great, in fact. Next Wednesday is her one-year anniversary of being cancer free. I just want to celebrate being together. Because, well hell, because I just cherish every moment we have, you know?"

I did know, and I told him so. "I can't offer you the jet any-more, but why don't you see what kind of flights you can get, and we can arrange for the island helicopter to ferry you over."

We work out the details, and I promise that if Dallas and I are still in LA we'll even hop to the island and visit. Then I hang up the phone, look at Dallas, and sigh.

"Hey," he says, taking my hands. "What is it?"

"I'm just so proud of both of them. The way they fought her cancer. The way they stood together. I don't know." I lift a shoulder. "We're fighting to survive, too, and I just hope we have the same strength together that Brody and Stacey do."

He pulls me into the circle of his arms and holds me tight. "Oh, baby, how can you doubt it? Think of everything we've been through. We've been forged in the fire, and we've come out stronger."

"Maybe," I say, as I press my cheek against his chest. "Maybe it doesn't matter?"

I feel him tense. "What do you mean?"

For just a moment, I lean back so that I can see his face. "Because sometimes the strong don't win, Dallas. We both know that. And I'm scared."

His brow furrows as concern flashes in his eyes. "Of what?"

"That no matter how hard we fight, it won't matter, and that somehow, someday, the world is going to rip us apart."

18

Sacrifices

She hoped he understood now.

Why she couldn't let anything or anyone get in their way.

Why she had to clear a path for them to be together.

Why she had to make him understand that everything would be okay once he left that little bitch. Once he was hers again.

She hadn't wanted to hurt the dog, but she'd looked in his eyes and known that he understood. Animals often had that connection with humans, dogs especially. They sacrificed fully. Willingly. All in the effort to please.

Why couldn't humans do the same? Why couldn't they see?

Hell, why couldn't he see?

Over and over she'd tried to get his attention. To change his course. And yet still he was unswayed.

But she wasn't beaten, not yet.

If he wasn't seeing her, she'd just have to up her game.

She knew how to do that. All she had to do was wait for just the right moment . . .

19

Breaking Bad

"The whole situation is just horrible," Nikki says as she digs into one of Flamingo Grille's famous gingerbread pancakes. It's one of my favorite West Hollywood restaurants, and when Nikki called this morning after she heard the news about that poor dog, Dallas suggested they join us for breakfast since Dallas and I are catching an afternoon flight back to New York. I'd been a little hesitant at first, as my melancholy from last night still lingered, but I can't deny that it's nice to see them and talk about what happened.

"And you said you're pretty sure the dog's owner isn't the one who did it?" she continues. "Even though she posted all those nasty tweets about Dallas?"

"She's been out of the country for weeks," Dallas said. "I just got confirmation this morning."

Under the table, Dallas takes my hand. Quince had used his MI6 connections to track down Carol Lucas's various comings and goings through her passport number, and had learned she'd been traveling through Europe for the past fourteen days, with her dog tucked away in one of Los Angeles's many doggy spas.

Of course, the call from Quince hadn't really changed anything as far as I was concerned. Both Dallas and I were already convinced that the Woman is my stalker. But, Nikki and Damien know none of that.

"I'm sorry you're leaving town so soon," she continues. "I was hoping we could spend some time. But I'd do the same thing in your shoes, and I imagine you'll feel a lot safer in an apartment with a doorman than in a rather secluded house."

"Very true," I admit. "Plus, I really just want to be close to my mom." Another truth, because even if Dallas and I didn't need to bring both our parents up to speed, I'd still want to be near my mother.

Nikki's smile flickers. "I've never had a crisis where I actually wanted my mother. In fact, given the option, I'd run as far and as fast as possible."

"I'm sorry," I say, but she just shakes her head as Damien takes her hand.

"Thanks, but it's fine." Nikki smiles at him. "Actually, it's perfect."

Since I've obviously touched on a sore spot, I struggle to find a new subject, then land on Hollywood and my script and Lyle Tarpin—who Nikki has actually met a few times—and then other random subjects like vacation homes and travel plans and who makes the best cocktail in Los Angeles.

In other words, perfectly normal stuff.

Throughout the meal, Damien's phone has vibrated on the table with a dozen or so text messages. He never responds, keeping his focus instead on us and the conversation, which I find particularly polite, considering the empire he controls.

This time when he glances down, though, he doesn't immediately ignore the text. Instead, he frowns as he reads it, then looks between Dallas and me. "This is from my media people. It looks limited right now, but my guess is it'll go viral within the hour."

Without even thinking about it, I've reached for Dallas and am clutching his arm so hard it's a wonder he has circulation. I can feel him beside me, as tense as I am.

"Just spit it out, man," Dallas says, the dread clear in his voice.

Damien draws a breath, then passes us his phone. It's open to a text message.

Re: Resort at Cortez Negative PR. Mr. Stark, I regret to tell you that the attached has just broken. Since it involves a Cortez investor, I wanted you to see it ASAP.

Beneath the message is a tiny icon representing a photograph. Dallas taps on it, and it enlarges to fill the phone's screen.

Sex in Captivity!
The now-disinherited Sykes heirs Jane Martin and Dallas Sykes have been in the news lately because of their sexy sibling shenanigans. But new information suggests these two have a long history—and that they even lost their virginity to each other while the victims of an unreported kidnapping, captive fifteen-year-olds awaiting ransom. Truth or terrible rumor? We can't wait to find out!

My stomach clenches, and for a moment I think I'm going to be ill. I'm still holding tight to Dallas's arm, and I keep my eyes down, my gaze focused on the remains of my Spanish omelet until I feel steady enough to look up. I'm certain that Nikki or Damien are going to ask about the kidnapping even if they don't take the extra step to pry into our sexual relationship.

But to their credit, neither says a thing, and all I see when Nikki looks at me is a compassion so genuine that my entire body sags with relief.

"Jane?" Dallas uses his free hand to peel off my still-tight fingers. He holds my hand and looks hard at my face. I can see his own fury, banked by his concern for me.

"I'm okay," I say. "Just caught off guard." I make a face. "And dreading the vultures that are going to be camped out in front of our apartment when we get home."

"Then don't go home," Nikki says. "At least not yet. Take another day here."

"The house will be worse," Dallas points out. "Easier access. The street is probably already a nightmare."

"Then go stay on the island." Damien says, referring to The Resort at Cortez, and Dallas's bungalow there.

"Exactly," Nikki says. "Stay out of the public eye and regroup. Even if just for twenty-four hours."

"It won't die down in a day," I say, but my protest is hollow. I want what she's suggested. Time away from the madness. Time with Dallas.

I want it, yes. More important, I think we need it.

"You're right," Nikki says. "It won't go away that fast. But the initial wave of mania will be over. More important, you'll be in a better place. Go to the island. Ignore your phones, your computers, the Internet."

I glance at Dallas, and I know he can see the question in my expression. *Can we? We said we'd tell our parents everything. Can we wait another day?*

"I think they're right," Dallas says. "I think we should take a day."

I nod, so overwhelmed with relief that I feel as if I would float to the ceiling if Dallas released my hand. Because I don't want to face my mom and dad with this news so raw, like an open wound on our family. I need time to think. To heal. To just be with Dallas before the madness starts.

Then reality hits me like a pin, and I deflate a bit. "We still have to go by the house. All our stuff is there."

"Tell me what you need and I'll send someone to get it. Or I can have a security team escort you home. Whatever you need."

"Thanks," Dallas says. "We'll take you up on that."

"Yes," I agree. "We really—oh, hell. I forgot about Brody and Stacey." I glance between Nikki and Damien. "We just offered the bungalow to my best friend and his wife. They're coming in today."

"So you guys can stay in ours," Nikki says. "Better yet, put your friends up there. And stay in your own place."

"Are you sure?" Stacey is a huge tennis fan, and Damien played professional tennis until he quit to found an empire. For her, the idea of staying in Damien Stark's bungalow is the equivalent of telling a kid they get to ride in Santa's sleigh.

"It's our pleasure," Damien says.

"Just go," Nikki adds. "Enjoy your friends. Relax. And for just a little while, try to escape the world."

20

Lovers & Friends

"Stacey wants it to be officially known that she is in heaven sleeping in Stark's bedroom," Brody says as we walk barefoot along the private beach in the island's gated area. "Personally, I think that's just a little kinky. But since I'm good with kink, I'm going to roll with it."

I bump him with my shoulder. "You're a good husband."

"That's what I keep telling her. Seriously, thanks for getting us the bungalow. And thanks for giving Stark her email address. The email from him and Nikki telling us where various things are in the bungalow and assuring us we should make ourselves at home was a nice touch. And I'm pretty sure Stacey's going to print it out and frame it once we get back to New York."

"Not a problem. And Nikki really wanted to reassure you both that you were welcome."

He and Stacey had arrived about an hour ago, and we met them at the helipad. We showed them to the Stark bungalow and gave them the quick and dirty tour of the island, pointing out important features like the small but well-stocked liquor store, the restaurant, and the spa.

Then Stacey went inside to unpack while Dallas went into our bungalow to make some phone calls. At least, that's what they said. Brody and I both knew they were just giving us time to catch up.

"I'm so glad you're here," I say honestly. "I miss you. I haven't seen you since . . ." I trail off. The sun is too bright, the beach is too pretty, the sky is too blue. I just don't want to think about what happened.

"Since the bitch attacked you?" Brody says, clearly not reading my mind.

"It's been a little hectic since then," I say dryly.

"I was a fucking basket case, you know that, right? Your mom told you? I mean, I get why they wanted to be careful, but I was really freaked."

I reach for his hand and squeeze it. "I missed you, too."

He shoots me a sideways look. "So how are you doing? Really?"

I frown as I think about it. "I feel exposed. Raw. And vulnerable. I mean, she just came out of the dark and attacked me. And then to do that to a dog." I shiver, then hug myself.

"And Dallas?"

Just his name makes me smile. "He makes me feel safe." It's a simple answer, but the truth often is, and that is the most basic truth between us: we make each other feel safe.

"I'm glad to hear it, but what I meant is how's he doing? With the attack on you, I mean. And also with the news that just hit the papers."

I make a face. "You saw. Great, huh? Pretty soon they'll offer us a reality TV show."

"Good girl," Brody says, then shrugs when I aim a questioning look his way. "I just think you have to keep your sense of humor about that. Not about the stalker, but the tabloids? Fuck it, you'll never get ahead. At any rate, you didn't answer my question. How's Dallas handling everything? Especially the attack on you and this horror with the dog?"

"He's feeling furious," I admit. "Not to mention impotent."

Brody's brows rise, and I roll my eyes. "No, we're going fine in that department," I say. "Problem pretty much solved there."

"Also glad to hear it."

"I just mean that he wants to jump in and be my protector, but he doesn't know who to protect me from."

"You guys don't have any idea at all?"

"We're convinced it's the Woman," I say, then shrug. "But who the hell is she?"

"Someone you've seen before."

"Well, yeah. I saw her in a cell seventeen years ago."

He shakes his head. "No, I mean she's not just going to pop out of the woodwork after that much time."

"Agreed. Dallas and I talked about that. She's been watching all this time. Honestly, it's creepy."

"I'll say."

I bend down to pick up a shell, then toss it back into the ocean. "What did you say a few seconds ago?"

"That she won't just pop out of the woodwork?"

I shake my head. "No. You said that we've seen her before." I tap my finger on my chin as I think, as if that will jar my thoughts into place. "That's so obvious, but I never thought of it like that. I thought about her watching us. Not us seeing her. But we've probably noticed her. Maybe even talked to her."

"Maybe at one of Dallas's famous parties."

I roll my eyes. "Well, great. We've just narrowed the suspect list down to ninety-five percent of the female population of Manhattan."

"Yeah, but you can narrow it down more. Most of the girls at those parties are just that. Girls. But if your attacker is the Woman, she has to be older, right?"

"True. But there were a lot of older women vying for the chance to cheat on their husbands with Dallas." I twist my mouth wryly. "I'm pretty sure they even formed a Meetup group."

Brody ignores me. "She could also be someone in the neighborhood. Not necessarily a resident. But the dry cleaner. Or even one of Dallas's part-time maids or cooks. After the kidnapping, she worked her way into his life. She wants to be close to him. Hell, she *has* to."

"But if I'm her competition, why didn't she just kill me on the street? She could have easily." It's true. I hate it, but it's true.

"Who knows? Maybe you're just lucky. Maybe she's got something that passes for a conscience. Or maybe she just likes the drama that comes with playing a game."

"The drama," I say, feeling a little sick. I remember how she was when she tied me down so she could go torture Dallas. I recall what Dallas has told me about what she did to him, the sick games she made him play. The way she got off on it.

"You nailed it," I say, meeting Brody's eyes. "She's definitely playing a game."

"I know." His voice is low, as serious as I've ever heard it. "Let's hope to hell she loses."

21

Perspectives

Dallas stood on the back porch looking out at the Pacific, breathing in the sea air and listening to the waves crash onto the beach. In the distance, he could see Brody and Jane returning, and he watched their progress. The view was peaceful, even beautiful, and it pissed him off that they'd come to this perfect location not for a romantic getaway but as an escape from a tabloid hell. Not to mention a damn stalker.

Fucking bullshit.

On the beach, Brody veered off toward the Stark bungalow, and Jane picked up speed until she was jogging toward Dallas.

"Hey," she said, peering at his face. "We've got this. We can handle this."

He lifted a brow. "Handle it? Our deepest secrets spewed all over the goddamn media like it's entertainment?"

For a moment, she just stared at him. Then she surprised the hell out of him and burst out laughing. She was laughing so hard, in fact, that she had to back up and lean against the wall.

"Christ, Jane." He practically growled the words. But the more she laughed—the more she held up her hand to indicate that she just couldn't talk yet—the more he calmed down. And by the time he actually pulled her still-hiccupping body into his arms, he was actually smiling. Although that was more in response to her than to any humor in the situation.

"Talk to me," he said, when she finally relaxed in his arms.

She tilted her head back, her eyes lit with amusement. "I'm sorry. I'm sorry. But come on, Dallas. Our secrets are already all over the media. We already are entertainment. And hell, maybe all the idiots who've been saying we're vile will take a step back now that they know more about what happened."

"Do you want them to know more?"

She shook her head. "No—god no. I want this all to go away. But . . ."

"But what?"

"It's not going to go away. We're stuck with the cameras and the gossip and it's horrible, but it's there."

"I know," he said. "But that's not the point."

"Then what is?"

He shook his head, then took a step back as he ran his fingers through his hair, trying to gather his thoughts. Hell, trying to fully understand his reaction himself. Because the truth was, she was right. This was just one more thing. One more burden. One more bone for the media dogs to chew on.

Except this wasn't about the media. This was about them. Or, more specifically, it was about the spotlight always shining on them. And not because Jane looked hot in a gown when she walked down the red carpet at some Hollywood charity event. Not even because Dallas was rumored to be fucking the latest A-list actress, not anymore anyway.

On the contrary, the gossip centered around their doomed relationship. A brother and a sister in love and disinherited. A tragedy played out across the Internet.

And every screen impression, every headline, every mention on some celebrity gossip show shouted out to the world that the way Dallas and Jane felt about each other was doomed. And worse.

Wrong.

Dirty.

Sinful.

She was the best part of his life, and yet all that the world reflected back to them was dirt and shame. Even in his own goddamn family.

And he fucking hated that.

Roughly, he took her hand and pulled her hard to him. She gasped, stumbling a little. He could see the question in her eyes and so he claimed her mouth before she could avoid it. The kiss was hard, almost desperate. It was a magic potion, a ticket, a window to a world without his dark thoughts, his taunting frustrations. A world where it was just Dallas and Jane. Love without all the goddamn strings and hurdles.

"I need you," he whispered as he broke the kiss long enough to pull her tank top over her head. She wore nothing under it, and now she stood before him in just a pair of running shorts, her breasts heavy and her skin flushed. Her lips plump from kissing. She stood with her legs slightly spread, and he idly rubbed his thumb and forefinger together, imagining how slick she was, how sweet she'd taste. His cock, already rock hard inside the cheap pair of athletic shorts he'd tossed on as soon as they'd arrived at the bungalow, throbbed almost painfully.

Roughly, he tugged her head to the side, making her gasp. Then he kissed his way down the side of her throat, relishing the small noises she made as she grew more and more needy.

"Tell me," he demanded as he kissed her lower still, then flicked his tongue over her nipple. "Tell me you know that you're mine." He bit her nipple as he slid his fingers down into her shorts and under her panties, moaning at just how wet she was.

"Yes." Her word was barely a moan. "Yes, Dallas, I know. Oh, god!" The word ripped out of her as he thrust his fingers inside her, and her muscles clenched tighter around him.

"Tell me you want me to fuck you." He moved his fingers in and out, brushing her clit with each long, deep stroke.

"*Yes*. Please, please, Dallas. Yes."

"Oh, holy hell." He'd wanted to tease her. To make it build. But there was so much pure need in her voice that he couldn't wait any longer. He had to be inside her.

He pulled his fingers from her, eliciting a frustrated groan. But that turned quickly into a gasp when he yanked down her shorts and panties. "Step out of them," he said, and as soon as she complied, he cupped his hands around her ass and lifted her. "Ride me," he demanded. "Hook your legs around my hips and ride my cock."

He held her weight as she lowered herself so that the tip of his cock teased her pussy. And it was all he could do not to come right then. Christ, he wanted to be inside her, and for just a moment the fear that he would lose his erection tormented him. *Fuck no*. Not now. Not tonight.

And as if he had to prove the point, he took a step forward so that part of her weight was supported by the side of the house, then urged her body lower, impaling her fully on his cock.

"Kiss me," he demanded, then took her mouth roughly, his tongue warring with hers, as hot and hard and wild as the thrusts of his cock. "Touch yourself," he told her when he could feel her body tightening. She was close, so close, and he wanted to feel her explode around him. He wanted her to completely shatter in his arms. "Slide your hand between us and stroke your clit."

She did, and he kissed her again, tugging on her lip, diving deep with his tongue. Teasing the corner of her mouth even as the rhythmic motion of her hand on her clit set his skin on fire, the way her fingers brushed over him simply from the proximity of their bodies.

"Tell me you're close," he said, when he knew he couldn't last much longer.

"Yes." Her voice was like a breath. "God, yes."

"That's it, baby. Come for me." He felt her body tighten around his cock, the way her legs shook with mounting pleasure, and her satisfaction pushed him to the edge. "*Now*," he cried. "Oh, god, Jane, *now*."

She tightened around him as he exploded inside her, and they rode the wave together, hard and deep, until they both stopped trembling and his legs couldn't take it anymore and they slid, sated and helpless, to the porch.

They stayed there, breathing hard, for what felt like hours, but was really only minutes. Then she shifted and propped herself up on her elbow. "That was incredible," she said. "You gonna tell me what started it?"

"Maybe you just drove me a little wild in that cute top."

"Uh-uh. Try again."

"Take a wild guess."

She sighed. "Fuck the world, Dallas. What is it to us?"

He cocked his head. "You really believe that?"

She considered the question, then sighed as she shook her head. "No, but I'm trying to believe it. But come on, Dallas, you've been living like the poster boy for hedonism for years. Some of this should be familiar."

"It is," he admitted. "And it's not the attention per se that bothers me. It's what they say about us. And honestly, I think I could stand even that if only—" He cut himself off.

"Mom's behind us," she said softly, because of course she

knew where he'd been heading. "And maybe Dad will come around in time."

"I'm not going to bet the ranch."

Her brow rose. "We have a ranch?"

He bit back a laugh, then took her hand and pulled her close, and held her in the circle of his arms.

"At any rate, I guess it is more than just Mom and Dad. Maybe I just don't like to share our history with the world." He kissed her softly, thinking that he could hold her like this forever. "You were my dirtiest secret, down there in the dark where nobody knew."

"But they do know. So what does that make me?"

"Now you're my sweetest taboo."

Laughter danced in her eyes. "Good," she said, "because you're mine, too."

He pulled her to her feet and led her inside where they both laid down, sprawling lengthwise on the couch. He breathed in, calmed by the fresh, familiar scent of her shampoo. "Adele was right," he said thoughtfully. "She predicted that someone would eventually leak the whole sex-in-captivity thing, and she was one-hundred-percent fucking right. But in a way this is good."

"Good? How?"

"It proves what we've already suspected. That Colin's been lying about the Woman being dead. She's not dead, she's very much alive. She's the leak, baby. The only other people who know are people we trust. Which means that if we can trace the leak back to its source, we've got her. All we need now is time."

The next morning, Dallas looked out at the great ocean that filled his vision. He was barefoot, and the sand felt cool and firm beneath his feet, and yet each time the waves tumbled in, the foundation below him shifted a little. Maybe not enough to knock him down, but enough so that he had to keep readjusting his balance.

And wasn't that a metaphor for his life?

Here on the island, everything was perfect. But they couldn't stay here, and soon he and Jane were going to have to go back to the real world.

Dammit, he wasn't ready. He'd never be ready until he knew Jane would be safe.

He drew a breath and pushed the thoughts from his mind. Then he stood a few more moments, simply enjoying the sound of the surf, the smell of the salt water. A pair of seagulls dive-bombed the water just past where the waves broke, and when one emerged with a wriggling fish, the other cawed in either approval or irritation that it had failed to get breakfast as well.

He was facing west, and so the sunrise was less vibrant, but still dramatic. The gray of dawn had succumbed to a deep blue that was now cut through by bands of gold and yellow and orange, all of which would give way to a vibrant sky blue as the hour grew later.

Dallas glanced at his watch and shifted his feet out of the pockets of sand into which he had sunk. He'd gone out on a mission to bring back breakfast tacos, but the morning had been so clear that he'd decided to walk the long way to the restaurant, following the beach from his private backyard all the way around to the main resort area.

He'd thought about waking Jane to join him, but she'd looked too peaceful. Better to rouse her gently with breakfast. And maybe even a mimosa. Surely he could grab a bottle of champagne from the restaurant.

Besides, he wanted to catch up with Liam and the guys. And that was a conversation he didn't want to have in front of Jane.

Not that he intended to keep the investigation into her attack from her, but this island was supposed to be about escaping, not about reliving the horror.

Escaping. He smiled a little to himself as he walked. That was true. He'd come here wanting to escape everything. Everything, that is, except Jane. He could never escape her, even if he wanted to. She was the key to his life, to his heart. Hell, maybe even to his sanity.

She'd told him that she would go into the dark with him, and that promise had the power to drop him to his knees. But what he was starting to realize was that he didn't need the dark anymore. All he needed was her. All of the other shit that he'd craved fizzled away when she was around, no match for the pure intensity of what he felt for her.

Sure, he still enjoyed sex rough. Still got hard at the thought of knowing that she would bend to his will. That she would give herself over to his enjoyment and, more, that he was responsible for hers. That she was surrendering everything to him. That she was trusting him completely.

But it wasn't kink that he craved—it was Jane. The pleasure of feeling her against him. The heat of her skin. The allure of her touch. Wild, gentle, rough, easy. He wanted it all. Hell, with Jane he craved it. Needed her touch, the way she gave herself over to him, as much as he needed to breathe. Not as punishment, but as pleasure. As a gift for the both of them, every intimate act taking them higher and making them closer.

And yes, they both still fought their demons—hell, they probably always would—but for the most part, they'd weathered the storm.

Pretty fucking amazing.

And yet there was still a hole in his heart. Because no matter how much they'd conquered and how much they overcame, at the end of the day, they couldn't be together. He would never stand at an altar and watch her come toward him in a white dress. He'd never see their grandmother's face light up as they cut the cake at their reception. He'd never see Jane dance the first dance with their father.

And he'd damn sure never see Eli give her away to him.

Fuck.

He wanted those things—he did. But he knew well enough that they'd never be his.

His phone buzzed, and he stopped walking as he pulled it from his back pocket, expecting Jane. Instead, he realized that a call from Liam had gone to voicemail and he brought the phone up to his ear, listening to Liam's update as he walked.

In the message Liam ran through all the dead ends. The attempts to track who might have released Carol Lucas's dog from the kennel. The update on searching for the van in various security and traffic camera footage in an attempt to get a photograph of the driver and passenger. Quince's progress with Colin, which was pretty damn minimal. In other words, nada.

"That's pretty much it," Liam's message continued. "We're still pulling at threads. Analyzing the paper those letters to you were written on. Comparing guest lists to all your parties over the years and checking the names against their social media accounts to see if any crazy shows up. But it's not going to be fast. We're dealing with an extremely intelligent psychopath. So watch your back. And take care of Jane."

Dallas frowned, wishing the news were better. He started to type out a text response to Liam, then decided not to. Liam hardly needed Dallas's input, and for one more day Dallas craved escape.

When he looked up, the women on the beach had gotten close enough to recognize, and he waved. The tall brunette with the vibrant tattoo of a bird on her arm and shoulder was Cass, Sylvia's best friend. Sylvia was Stark's former assistant and now the project manager for The Resort at Cortez. But it wasn't Syl who walked beside Cass, but a lean redhead who he recognized as her girlfriend, Siobhan.

"I didn't realize you two were on the island."

Cass shook her head. "We weren't supposed to be here at all. Syl and Jackson had intended to come last night with the kids for a few days of R & R, but then Jeffery got an ear infection, so they're staying home." She reached for Siobhan's hand and grinned. "Worked out well, though. No better place to celebrate than here, right?"

"What are you celebrating?"

As if they'd both been waiting for him to ask the question, they each thrust out their left hands, revealing matching silver bands ringed with Celtic symbols. "You got married. That's wonderful. Congratulations."

"Not yet. But we did get engaged."

"She popped the question," Siobhan added, grinning. "Got down on her knees and everything, it was totally corny and incredibly awesome."

"I didn't have a ring, but I didn't want to wait. We were playing miniature golf of all things, and she just looked so perfect."

"So she used one of the hoops from her ear," Siobhan continued. "It didn't even really fit, but I wore it anyway on the tip of my pinkie until we could go buy matching rings." She lifted Cass's hand to her lips and kissed it. "And so here we are."

"When's the date?"

"Haven't set it yet. You'll come?"

"Wouldn't miss it."

They exchanged glances. "Is Jane here?"

He felt his gut tighten. Cass had never met Jane, but the fact that she knew of her made it all too clear that she'd seen the media reports. "She's back at the bungalow."

"Oh, good. We'd love to meet her." Once again, she took Siobhan's hand. "Listen, I hope this isn't out of line, but I just want to say I feel for you. I mean, you should be able to be with the person you love, you know?"

Wasn't that the god's honest truth?

And as he watched them walk away, he realized that maybe—just maybe—he'd finally figured out how. Even if his father continued to refuse to help.

22

Eternity & Back

Dallas has set up a small picnic on the private section of the beach that makes up our bungalow's backyard. Since I'm in full picnic mode, I'm wearing a little black bikini that was definitely designed to soak up a maximum amount of sun. I have a sarong tied at my waist, but it's for fashion more than coverage, as the slit at the side reveals more than a little hip and one entire thigh.

Dallas is dressed casually, too, in khaki shorts and a white short-sleeved Henley that accentuates both his tan and the toned muscles of his arms. Honestly, the picnic is nice, but I'd be content to just lay here and soak up the view.

A blanket serves as our dining area, and we're enjoying an incredible lunch of fresh fruit and stuffed fillets of salmon that Dallas actually made himself. I take a bite, then sigh with pleasure before taking another sip of my wine mixed with Diet Sprite, a drink Dallas thinks is the devil, but I think is totally refreshing and beach-worthy.

Dallas meets my eyes, and for some reason I laugh.

"All right," he says. "Tell me."

"I don't know what's funny. Maybe I'm just grateful I have a boyfriend who can cook."

"Boyfriend," he says, as if he's turning the word over and examining it from all sides. "I don't think you've called me that before."

I lift a shoulder as cold fingers of discontent edge toward me. "Well, it's true."

"Very true," he says, and the heat in his voice is undeniable.

"I want more." My confession is soft, and I toy with the stem of my wineglass as I say it. "I don't know, Dallas. I want to say I'm not pissed at Daddy for not agreeing with your idea about rescinding, but I am. He just doesn't see the big picture. And you and I—we've lost out on so much time already."

For a moment he just looks at me, then he gets up and kneels in front of me, his hands on the arms of my beach chair so that I'm locked in and he's very, very close. "I love you," he says.

"You better," I counter.

His lips don't even twitch, and his eyes don't drift off mine. "I love you," he says again, extending his hand. "Come with me."

Since I really have no choice in the matter, I do, and he leads me all the way down to where the ocean greets the waves as they roll in and roll out in a timeless rhythm.

I'm about to ask him again what we're doing, but he pulls me close and kisses me, hard and deep and so passionately it seems as though that kiss has released a thousand strings of firelight that are now lighting me up from the inside.

I whimper when he pulls away, because although I want him to tell me what's on his mind, I also don't want that kiss to end.

"Tell me you can't live without this," he says.

"You know I can't."

"Tell me you want me."

"I do," I whisper. "You know I do."

"I did some thinking on the beach today and I realized that I don't want to wait anymore. So I went to the gift shop, and I bought you something."

I'm about to ask what he's talking about when he actually drops to one knee in front of me, then holds up a blue-green macramé ring. It's so absurd—and yet his face is so serious—that tears well in my eyes and I press my fingers to my mouth.

"Marry me, Jane."

A tear escapes, and I taste its saltiness when I open my mouth to gasp. "Dallas, what—"

"I love you," he interrupts. "I've loved you for as long as I can remember, and I will love you for the rest of my life and beyond. I don't want to spend a day without you. You inspire me. You humble me. You're my best friend and my deepest passion. The other half of me. The best part of my soul. Please, Jane Martin. Will you be my wife?"

I'm not sure when it happened, but somehow I'm on my knees, too, and he's slipping the silly ring on my finger, and I'm hugging it to my chest, the tears coming too hard and too fast for me to manage words.

I want to pull him close and kiss him hard; I want to shake him and demand to know what the hell he's been smoking.

I'm bursting with sunshine; I'm completely miserable.

I love him—and yet we both know I can't have him. And I don't understand why he's playing such a cruel game, teasing us both with something that is so far out of reach.

He cups my cheek. "Say something, baby. If it's the ring, I promise I'll take you to Tiffany when we get back home."

Laughter escapes, conquering the building tears. "No way," I say. "I love this ring. It's just that I—I don't know why you're doing this. We can't—you know we can't. There's no state—no country, even—where we can get married, and if Daddy won't agree . . ."

"All the more reason for us to go ahead and do it."

"You're talking crazy, Dallas."

"I'm talking about you and me." He brushes the tears from my cheek with the side of his thumb. "Maybe we are a little crazy, but I want to do this."

"Do what?" I know my voice sounds exasperated but I feel like a child who's been shown the most delectable chocolate cake and yet it's forever just out of reach.

"I saw Cass and Siobhan on the beach this morning, and their engagement got me thinking about my friend Jared from St. Anthony's. Do you remember him?"

"The guy you and Quince used to study with? The one with the *Dr. Who* obsession?"

"That's him. He's gay, and about thirteen years ago, he and his partner, William, got married."

I frown. "Where were they living?"

"Chicago. He's an American like me. Just over there for the education."

"But—wait. Gay marriage hasn't been legal for that long. Not even close."

"They did it themselves. Had a ceremony with friends, and it was nice. Quince and I were both there. Had estate planning papers drawn up. Not a state-sanctioned marriage, a do-it-yourself one."

"Oh," I say, finally understanding where he's going with this.

"So we have a service. We revise our wills. We draft a partnership agreement. We hire a lawyer and make the estate part of this work. The rest of it is just you and me deciding to do it." He squeezes my hand. "And somewhere in all of that, I really will buy you a better ring."

I burst out laughing. "I love what you're suggesting. But, Dallas, it's not the same, and they still win, and—"

"No," he says, shaking his head. "That's the point. They

don't win. *We* do. Because we're changing the rules. We're taking control from the people who deign to say what we can be to each other. And we'll be together. Say, yes, baby. Say yes, and be my wife."

"Yes," I say, then throw my arms around him as a joyous laughter bubbles out of me. "Yes, yes, a million times, yes."

And then he's kissing me, and we fall backward on the sand, and the surf splashes up over us so that I squeal and try to squirm away, but he holds me down tight, his hands pinning me at the wrists as he straddles my waist.

"And you know the best part?" he says with a playful grin.

"The sex?"

He grins, but otherwise ignores me. "If we ever sell our story, you can write it."

"That's not the best part," I counter. "The best part is that we have a happy ending."

"Yeah," he says, looking at me with such tenderness I almost melt. "We do."

I'm still trapped beneath him, but as another wave comes in, I gasp from the cold and then wiggle my hips. "And meanwhile, we still have the sex."

His mouth twitches. "Oh, yeah," he agrees. "We definitely do."

He stands, then scoops me up, surprising me by hoisting me over his shoulder and giving my ass a light slap. "Dallas!" I squeal, but the protest is only for show. Wherever he's taking me, I'm going willingly. I just don't want to go far.

Neither does he, and he puts me down carefully on the blanket after just a few steps. "Here?" I ask, a little breathless.

"Here. Now. Because I don't want to go another step without being inside you. I want the blue sky above us and the heat of the sun rivaling the way the touch of your skin burns through me."

He's still standing, and I enjoy the view of his damp T-shirt and shorts clinging to his perfect body. He's hard, and I can see the outline of his cock against his shorts. He gets down beside me, and I prop myself up on one elbow as he leans in close to my ear and whispers softly so that his breath tickles my senses and sends shivers down my spine. "We've wasted time. But we're not going to waste any more."

"We're not?"

"Definitely not." His mouth brushes slowly over my cheek as he murmurs the words, and, dammit, I just can't take it any longer. I twist my head, forcing my mouth against his, and then sigh with pleasure when he opens to me.

He tastes like the Cabernet he's been sipping, and I'm so light-headed from the way his tongue is teasing me that I think perhaps I'm drunk on him, and I moan a little, letting him in deeper and losing myself in the taste and touch of him.

I'm aching for him, desperate to feel his hands on me. I crave the warmth of his skin against mine and the weight of his hips on my pelvis. I crave that sweetness of a building climax as he teases me softly, stroking tender areas, playing me like an instrument that he is building to a bold crescendo.

I crave it, and yet so far, I don't have it, though I can't complain about the wonders he's performing with his mouth. First teasing my lips, then peppering kisses up my cheek.

Now, his teeth nip at the lobe of my ear, and I feel the tug all the way down to my sex. I press my legs together, desperate to quell this building craving. And yet that's not the kind of satisfaction I want. So instead I change tactics, and as his tongue sweeps the curve of my ear, sending shivers coursing through me, I ease my own hand down under the band of my bikini bottom and slide my finger over my very wet pussy. I close my eyes, losing myself in the feel of Dallas's tongue on my ear—and my fantasy that it's his fingers stroking me. Teasing me. Dipping just barely inside my folds, and then—

His firm grip closes around my wrist and I open my eyes to

the realization that he is no longer nibbling on my ear. On the contrary, he's glaring down at me, his expression stern, and at the same time amused.

"Oh, no," he says. "No unauthorized touching."

"Is that the game?" I ask innocently. I spread my legs as wide as possible and look up at him with wide eyes. "Well, in that case, why don't you take over for me?"

"No."

I blink. That really wasn't the answer I was expecting. "No?"

"I want you to beg," he says, and since I have no shame where Dallas is concerned I take his hand and press it to my crotch, then suck in a sharp breath. "Please. Oh, god, Dallas, please."

"Well, since you asked so sweetly . . ."

He rubs his thumb over my very soaked bikini until I am right on the edge. And only when he has me completely worked up does he slide his finger under the crotch and tease me mercilessly, setting off a storm of wild sensation inside me.

"Please," I say, squirming to take off the sarong.

"No." His hand on mine stops me.

My brow furrows. "What do you—"

But I don't get the question out because he covers my mouth with his finger, then unties the sarong with one hand while the other draws down the fly of his shorts. He urges me to lift my hips, then pulls the sarong free. Then slowly, without a word, he slides his hands up my body, leaving a trail of fire in his wake.

When he gets to my arms, he urges them above my head, then wraps the sarong around my wrists, tying them together. He meets my eyes, and there's no denying the heat, but it's tinged with a bit of humor, too.

"Mine," he says softly.

"Forever," I agree, as he keeps one hand on my bound wrists, then starts to kiss his way down my body. He uses his teeth to grab one of the small triangles of material that make up my bikini top, then yanks it aside so that my breast can pop free. I draw in a stuttering breath, then gasp with pleasure as his mouth grazes my breast.

He bites my nipple, and I arch up as the sweet sting curls through me, all the way to my sex. I squirm beneath him, wanting him there. His mouth on my pussy, his tongue on my clit. But he is taking his time, and I can't deny that even though his slow attention is excruciating, his progress from breast to cleavage and then down to my navel is wreaking havoc with my senses.

I spread my legs, my hips gyrating. I'm craving his touch—any touch—and even the warmth of the sun against the crotch of my bathing suit is erotic.

But it's not until his mouth reaches my bikini bottoms that I really lose my mind. Because that's when he takes his tongue and traces it along the soft crease of my thigh between my suit and my leg. I shiver and shake, nearly coming undone just from the fact that his magical tongue is so damn close—and yet not nearly close enough.

Once again, he uses his mouth to move aside my suit, and his teeth scrape my swollen, sensitive skin. A shiver cuts through me, and when he thrusts his tongue inside me, I cry out, screaming his name and begging him to please, please fuck me.

He lifts his head long enough to meet my eyes, his full of heat and mischief, and then he dives back down between my legs, licking and sucking and teasing my clit with such wild abandon that I'm certain that I will lose my mind before I orgasm and, finally, get some sweet relief.

I gyrate my hips. I'm panting. I'm wanting. Hell, I'm lost in the sensation of his tongue and the sun and the incredible pleasure of being taken here under the bright blue sky. And just when I think it will never end—just when I think that I will go mad balancing on this knife edge of pleasure—my body shudders one final time before everything explodes inside me and I shatter.

Dallas doesn't stop. He's relentless, milking my orgasm until I am quivering as the last electric sparks flutter through me. And that's when he releases my bound wrists. When he uses his fingers to pull aside my bathing suit crotch.

When he finally enters me hard and fast, I'm so turned on that I lift my hips to meet him, thrusting to match his rhythms, and gasping as pleasure builds and builds, this time deeper, hotter.

When he explodes inside me, I'm not far behind, and we both collapse, breathing hard beneath a sexual haze that still clings to us, as warm as the sun above and as bright as the clear blue sky.

And in that moment, in Dallas's embrace, I can't help but think that, at least for this small moment in time, everything is perfect.

That's an illusion, I know. But I cling to it. Savoring these moments before, inevitably, we have to return to the world.

23

Something to Talk About

Dallas and I hold hands as we wander The Resort at Cortez, going in and out of shops, sipping coffee in the shade, gazing with awe at the stunning paintings of ocean scenes that fill the fine art gallery. This is my first time on the island, and I'm having a wonderful time, despite the circumstances that drove us here.

After exploring the stores, we kick off our flip-flops and play in the fountain that is the centerpiece of the retail area. Jets of water shoot straight up inside a concrete circle in the middle of the common area, and I am soaked by the time we stop running around like idiots, trying to dodge the vertical spray.

A few other shoppers are scattered about, and they watch our antics. I think vaguely that I should be a little embarrassed by our silliness, but I'm honestly having too much fun. Besides, I'm engaged now. And that makes today a day to celebrate.

There's an ice cream stand by the fountain, and we both grab a cone, feeling light and alive, like children out discovering the world.

"Beach," he says, taking my free hand in his. "We're already soaked. Let's go make a sand castle."

"Two castles," I counter. "And mine is going to totally blow yours away."

"You can try," he says. "But you won't succeed."

I laugh out loud, thrown back suddenly to our childhood days on Barclay Isle, an island in the Outer Banks that has been in the Sykes family since the beginning of time.

I lick my strawberry ice cream cone and glance sideways at him. He'd opted for chocolate, and I laugh at the little mustache on his upper lip. I tug him to a stop, lean over, and lick the ice cream off. When I pull back, my pulse has kicked up a notch. "Tasty," I say.

"Very," he agrees, though I don't think he's actually talking about the ice cream.

"Did you plan to make this the perfect day, or did it just work out that way?"

"How could it be anything but perfect if we're together?"

His words are as soft as his expression, and I feel as melty as my ice cream. "Dallas," I begin, but I don't finish, because he's pulled me to him, and his lips brush mine, a sweet kiss made all the sweeter by the lingering taste of chocolate and strawberry.

"Oh, my gosh!"

I hear the words at the same time as I hear the clicking of cameras, and I pull back sharply.

Off to the side two twenty-something girls wearing island day passes are taking picture after picture.

I feel the heat rise to my cheeks—this isn't good.

I start to turn and walk away, but Dallas tugs me back so hard I drop my cone. It lands with a splat on the concrete at the same moment his lips crush mine. This time, there's nothing sweet about the kiss. It's hot and hard and demanding, and I feel the fire of his touch coursing through me. I want to lose myself in his arms, his kiss, his touch.

But then I remember where we are, and I jerk back with a start. "Dallas, no."

"Yes," he counters. "Goddammit, yes."

I search his face, so hard and determined. So full of need. And not just for me, but for something I don't recognize. Respect? Acceptance?

I'm not sure, but it doesn't matter, because I want him, too. I want to kiss him here by the fountain with the sun shining down on us and my heart full of him. So I do. I start to lean in again, but he anticipates me, grins wolfishly, and dives in to devour me.

And oh, dear lord, it's wonderful. The knowledge that he loves me. The freedom to show it in public, to say screw you to the world. This is how I want to live. Openly. Honestly.

Right in this moment, I feel as though I could soar.

And then those bitches go and ruin it all. "Too fucking hot, right?" one of them says in the kind of whisper that's meant to be heard. "Dallas, for sure, but together? I mean, I've never fucked a brother and a sister, but I'd give them a whirl."

"I've already had him once," the other says. "I met him at a wrap party for that movie I did two years ago. His tongue is magical, and his cock is huge. I sucked him off twice, you know. Wonder if she realizes she's getting my sloppy seconds. Not to mention half the female population's."

They both start to laugh—no, to *cackle*—and the sound rips through me like a goddamn chainsaw. I don't plan it—I really don't—but somehow I am out of Dallas's arms and across the short distance, and my palm is stinging because—holy shit—I just slapped the taller one hard across the cheek.

"You obnoxious little bitch," I snarl, even as the other one raises her camera and starts snapping away, capturing my fury, my stinging hand, and the shocked face of the bitch who'd supposedly been in Dallas's bed, with her hand against her cheek and her eyes wide with shock.

I really don't know how Dallas got us out of there. I was roiling too deep in shock and mortification, but somehow he managed, and when I stop seething, I realize that we're back in the bungalow and I'm breathing hard, still so furious that all I can think of is how much my hand still stings and how much I desperately want to smack her again.

I look at Dallas, expecting him to be the one to step in and calm me. I assume he's in a rational headspace because he so deftly led me home. But one look at his face and I realize that he's just as messed up as I am. Just as angry. Just as horrified.

Just as afraid we are never, ever going to be able to make this work.

I feel my body sag, defeat washing through me. It's hot and horrible, and I hate that two random women on the beach can erase all the pleasure I've gotten out of this day. Can make me second-guess my resolve to make what Dallas and I have together work despite all the odds stacked against us.

"Don't," he says as soon as we arrive. His voice is hard. Demanding.

"Don't what?"

"Don't doubt us."

"I'm not doubting," I lie. "They just pissed me off. They just made me—"

He grabs my wrists and tugs me toward him, so violently I lose my balance and end up at his feet on the hard tile floor. "Do you think I don't understand?" he rages. "That I don't see it on your face? Do you think I don't feel exactly the same way? That we're never going to get past this, and for the rest of our lives we're going to be objects of ridicule? Some goddamn joke on the Internet? A couple that teenagers make tasteless memes about? Do you think I want that?"

He grips my wrists tighter and pulls me up. "You don't, and I don't, but it's what we have and there's not a goddamn thing we can do about it."

I'm crying now, angry that I'm so upset. Frustrated that he feels as lost and violated as I do. And that's so goddamned unfair, because all that means is that I'm expecting him to take care of me. And, fuck it, I need to take care of myself.

Hell, I need to take care of Dallas.

I don't realize that I've made a decision until I fall back onto my knees and my fingers go to the button of his jeans, and then to the zipper.

"Jane . . ." His voice trails off, and I hear the warning. And the question.

I look up at him, trying to keep my expression innocent. "What? You don't want me to suck you off? To take you deep the way she did? You don't want to fuck my mouth, and then lay me out and fuck me hard?"

I reach into his briefs and close my hand around his shaft. He's hard and smooth against my palm, and I shift my hips as I kneel on my heels, realizing that I'm already wet. That I want this. I want wild. I want fucked up.

I want Dallas to fuck me hard, because I know that he wants it, too. More than that, I know that we both need it. Maybe that's pathetic. Maybe that's wrong. But I don't care. It's us. And he knows it as well as I do.

"Fucking you isn't going to make those bitches go away," he says. "It's not going to make it better."

"The hell it won't," I say. "You're angry because you feel like you can't protect me. Like this whole world is whipping around us like a cyclone, and you can't control it. You can't make it go away any more than you can keep it from hurting me. You saw me get pissed off. You saw me stumble. And you wanted to make it better. But you can't—not out in the world anyway. But in here, in this room, you can."

I draw a deep breath. "How many times have I told you I'd go into the dark with you? I meant it, Dallas. And maybe right now we need it."

"Oh, baby," he says, and there's something like resignation in his voice. "Do you have any idea how hard it makes me thinking about you tied up and helpless beneath me? About taking you hard, relentlessly? About fucking that pretty mouth while your hands are tied to your ankles, then bending you forward and grabbing your tits while I fuck you in the ass?"

I swallow, his words making me wet with anticipation. "Then do it," I demand.

"It's one hell of a fantasy, baby, but I don't need it anymore. I don't need the dark to get centered, not even after a run-in with the likes of those two bitches. It's you I need, not the kink."

His words crash through me, filling all my hollow places. But it's not enough. Not now. "If you need me, then take me," I demand. "Because maybe I *do* need it. But from you—only from you. I need it rough, Dallas. I need to push the envelope. I need—"

But I don't have to finish telling him because he pulls me to him with one hand, then grabs my breast with the other. The sundress I'm wearing is a halter style, and I'm wearing no bra, just the two triangular pieces of cotton that tie at my neck. He grabs the material and yanks, ripping the tie and making the top slide down, baring me from the waist up.

I gasp with surprise, then suck in air hard as he pinches my nipple between his fingers, spreading pain out like red hot threads that snap and spark and shift from tantalizing pain to the most potent of pleasure.

My mouth is another playground as he crushes his lips over mine, so hard they bruise me, so wild our teeth clash and I taste the coppery tinge of blood. It's a full-on assault of the senses, and I relish it. Hell, I need it.

But then as quickly as he claimed me, he pushes himself away, breathing hard. "Is that what you want?"

"Yes."

"Why?" The word is sharp. Serious.

I gape at him. "Did you not just see what happened? I fuck-ing lost it. I mean, I snapped, Dallas, and what those girls said is hardly the worst of what we're going to hear. So I need you. Because this is going to get bad. I need to know there's a place where I can let go. Where you will catch me. Bring me back even if I'm pushed to the edge."

I draw in a breath and rush on. "So I want it as hot and hard as you can make it. I want it rough. I want to be vulnerable. Because under it all, with you I know that I'm safe. I need—oh, god, Dallas, I need to feel. I need you to make me *feel*."

For a moment, he only looks at me, and this is one of the few times that I truly can't read his expression. I feel a sudden sharp pang of fear that somehow we've gotten off the same page, and that he doesn't get it. Doesn't get *me*.

But then he looks around the room, his gaze skimming the living and dining area. When he turns back to face me, his face is hard. Determined. And there is a very definite gleam in his eye.

"I think you need to go to the table, Jane. And I think you need to bend over."

The heat in his voice warms me, melting away the last of my trepidation. I do as he says, moving beside the dining table that is approximately one meter squared.

I glance back at him, uncertain where and how he wants me, but he makes a circular gesture with his finger, and I know to turn around and face the tabletop.

He comes up behind me, and presses his hand to the small of my back.

I shiver from his touch—and then cry out when he grabs the waist of the sundress and yanks hard, literally ripping it from my body. He does the same with my underwear, only they don't rip as easily, and there's a hard, hot pressure against my pussy before the material gives way.

The violent power of such a claiming act spins through my body. And, honestly, it's a wonder I don't come right then.

"Close your eyes," he says, and I comply, then spread my legs when he orders me to do that, too. "Wider," he says. "Even with the table legs."

That leaves me wide open and exposed. And when he wraps something around my ankles—"twine," he tells me—and ties me to the table legs, I feel the pounding of my pulse in my throat—and between my legs.

Because my legs are spread so far, I can bend forward and lay atop the table, my ass pretty much level with the tabletop. I know this, because that's exactly what Dallas has me do, and then he tells me to stretch my arms out in a V so that my fingertips hang over the opposite corners.

Dallas moves around the table to stand in front of me, and I lift my head and chest to look at him, my shoulders back as if I were in a kinky yoga class, tied down and doing the cobra pose.

"Like what you see?" he asks, smirking as he wraps one end of a length of twine around my wrist, then ties the other end to a table leg.

He's still wearing his jeans and T-shirt, and so I lift a brow and say, "Not bad. I can think of at least one way to improve my view."

"Can you?" He repeats the process with my other wrist so that I am now spread-eagled. Not to mention completely vulnerable.

He moves slowly around the table, trailing his fingertip over my skin as he moves. "Oh, sweetheart," he says. "I do like this. You're laid out like a feast for me."

"In that case, I hope you enjoy eating me."

I hear a muffled sound that may be him holding back a chuckle. "Oh, I'm very sure I will. Right now, though, this is about your enjoyment. Hold on."

His fingers leave my skin, and I feel bereft while he's not touching me. I try to twist around enough to find him, but it's just not possible, and I'm left to rely on my ears to tell me what he's doing. Honestly, I don't know. He's stepped into the bedroom and I hear him opening drawers, but I don't have a clue what he could be looking for.

Finally, he returns, and this time when his hands stroke my back, they are slick with oil. It heats up as he moves his palms over my shoulders and down my spine, and when I breathe in, I can actually taste the mint. "Massage oil," I say, and those simple words make me wonder what other sexual toys he might have here in the bungalow. Dallas invested in Cortez long before we got together, and I imagine he's brought a few of the women he fucked before me to the island.

"I have quite a few little treats stashed in the bungalow," he says, confirming my words and making my gut twist with jealousy. "But this is the first time I've used any of them with someone I love. With the only woman I've ever loved."

Immediately, my jealousy fades to warmth. I know with unerring certainty that what he says is true.

"I'd forgotten what was in this box, actually," he says. "Honestly, I have a pretty interesting collection."

"Oh, really?" I have no idea what interesting things he could be talking about—knowing Dallas, they could be anything. I don't ask, though. I'm quite certain that whatever it is, I'll find out soon enough.

Slowly, sensually, he strokes the oil over my back, my shoulders. Then he gets on the table and straddles me. The table is narrow, so it's a tight fit, and I close my eyes, relishing the way his thighs brush my waist and hips. The way the denim of his jeans rubs against my heated, sensitive skin.

I feel him shift, then shiver from the touch of his lips to my spine. It's so sweet and so sensual and so wonderfully erotic that I feel my core clench and I know that I'm wet.

He trails the kisses upward until he teases the back of my neck, and while his lips do a number on me there, his hands slide over my shoulders, slick and hot. He grasps my neck, and I bite my lower lip, wanting to feel more, to feel his grip tighten, to *submit*.

"You like that," he says.

"Yes."

He says nothing else, but he releases my throat, and I whimper in protest. Then he slides off me, and I want to cry with frustration, wondering if this is some sort of perverse punishment. But he is standing by the table, and this time I can see what he's doing—he's undressing. And I have to say, I very much like the view.

He turns to the side, and I hear the thud of something being laid on the table, but it's down near my legs, and I don't know what it is.

"What are you doing?" I ask.

"You said you wanted to feel," he says, but offers no other explanation.

After another moment, he is back on the table, his hands once more slick with oil. He straddles me again, only this time it's skin on skin, and when he slides his hands over my shoulders to my breasts, there's something in them. I glance down, then suck in air. "Dallas . . ."

"Trust me," he says. "Arch your chest up and close your eyes."

I do, but I also bite my lower lip as he attaches a wooden clothespin to each of my nipples.

"Okay?" he asks, and I make some sort of raw noise in my throat, because I'm not sure *okay* is exactly accurate.

Except after a moment, I realize I'm not biting down as hard. And the pain I'd felt has transformed into an intense warmth that I don't just feel in my breasts but throughout my body.

"I want you to feel everything," Dallas says, and I realize he's slowly moving down my back. Only this time, he's not stroking me with his hands. Instead, he's using something soft on my skin. A feather maybe. Or fringe?

It's not until he reaches my ass that I realize what it is he's teasing my skin with—a flail. And when he flicks it against my rear, I feel the connection all the way into my breasts.

He's doing what I asked—and damned if it doesn't feel glorious.

After a moment, he tosses the flail aside, and I wonder if he's done with me. Then I hear a telltale buzzing, and if I wasn't so aroused I would have laughed. As it is, I'm craving whatever he has planned.

Except he doesn't intend anything out of the ordinary with the vibrator. It's a small one, and he lifts my body just enough that he can put it under me so that it's not directly on my clit, but so that I feel the rumblings—along with the slow build of a growing pleasure.

As the vibrator teases me, he kisses his way up my inner thighs, the butterfly-soft touches so arousing that I feel swollen and needy. His tongue dips inside me, then his fingers, and then he finger-fucks me as I beg him to go deeper. To stand beside me and fuck me hard.

"Naughty girl," he says, then smacks my ass. I cry out, then moan with pleasure as he thrusts his fingers in deep. He rubs my ass to soothe it, then immediately spanks me again. I expect the same delight when he finger-fucks me, only this time, his fingers ease into my ass, and I just about lose it between that and the vibrator and these damned clothespins.

Over and over he repeats this sequence until I am a mindless blob of lust with only one thing in my mind—to be fucked. Hard and thoroughly. And I want it so badly, I'm willing to beg. Which I do.

"You want to be fucked?" he asks.

"Yes. Yes, please."

"Then tell me you're mine, Jane. Tell me that I'm the one you go to whenever it gets to be too much."

"I am. You are. God, oh god, Dallas, I can't—" It was too much. I couldn't take all of it. The onslaught of sensations. The wildness of the feelings crashing over me.

"Can't what?"

"Can't take it."

"You can, baby. You said you wanted to feel us. This is us. Raw connection. Primal need. You wanted to feel vulnerable, but it's not you who's vulnerable, it's me. Because you can destroy me with a glance. You can cut me down with a look. You can walk away from me, baby, and shatter my whole goddamn world."

His words are at least as powerful as his touch, and I tremble as another wave of desire crashes over me. And then almost weep with relief when he thrusts his cock deep inside me and starts to slowly pump me, his fingers twined in my hair, forcing me to arch up.

"Do you think I have the power because you're naked and tied down? Because I can spank your ass and use your body for my pleasure? Because right now I could do anything to you—anything—and you're helpless to stop me? Is that what you think?"

"Yes," I say, because I know that's the line I'm supposed to say.

"Well, you're wrong. Because you're everything to me, baby. You're the woman who fills me up. Who makes me whole. You're my reason to face the day, to go forward. You've shaped the man I am, Jane, and you'll shape the man I've yet to become. Everything good I owe to you, and right now I want you to do more than feel it. I want you to believe it. I need you, baby. Hell, we need each other. Tell me you know that, too."

"I do," I say as his body slams into mine.

"Tell me you won't leave me again."

"Never," I promise as he fucks me so deep I feel impaled upon him.

"I want you to come now. I want to feel your body claim me. Tightening around my cock and . . . Now, baby. Come for me now."

He smacks my ass one final time, then bends forward over me while still deep inside. Before I realize what he's doing, he takes the pins off my nipples, and a rush of blood returns. A rush that I feel not only in my nipples, but in my clit.

And that's where the world ends. I spin out of control, lost in the overwhelming wildness of the sensations that crash over me in wave after wave after wave, as powerful as the sensation of his palm against my ass. As wild as the words with which he brought me to my knees.

And in that moment, all my fears and worries fade away. I feel whole again. I feel loved.

He's right, I think as a deep exhaustion starts to settle over me. *He truly is mine,* I think. *And I am his. And together we can survive whatever comes.*

24

Right Before Your Eyes

Dallas was dreaming.

He knew it. He was asleep and he was dreaming and he was aware of that, but somehow, he couldn't wake up.

In fact, some instinct deep inside him was telling him not to wake up. That this was important. That this was a defining moment and if he woke, he'd lose everything.

And so he stayed in the dream. A dim room. An empty dining table. A single rose in a bud vase. And Jane in a sequined formal gown, her lips red and sultry, her eyes on him.

"Aren't you going to sit? I haven't finished telling you about what Brody said."

"Brody?"

"When we walked the beach."

You told me already, Dallas thought, some part of his mind remembering a conversation from before they'd fallen asleep. *You told me when I was awake.*

But he sat, and she sipped her wine. "The Woman isn't just

someone who's been watching us for years. She's someone we see all the time, too. Can you pass the bread?"

He looked down, and where there had been only a white linen tablecloth, there was now a silver breadbasket.

He passed it, and she took a roll. "It's a subtle distinction, but it's important. She's in our lives." She shrugged. "Or maybe she isn't. How can we know?"

"Clues," Liam said from the third chair. "I'm looking for clues just like you asked me to. Only sometimes clues are easy to miss." He was wearing a blindfold, and took it off. "Much easier this way."

"What am I not seeing?" Dallas asked, but no one answered.

A waitress came and refilled his wineglass, then bent close and whispered, "It could be me."

"What?" He whipped around to look at her, but she was gone. When he looked back, so was Liam. But he saw something in the wine. A face? But it was gone before he could identify it.

Then the wine was gone along with the table, and suddenly he was at the Meadow Lane house he grew up in, standing by the pool with a woman on each arm.

"I've been to every party you've thrown," said the redhead.

"So have I," said the brunette.

"Could it be us?" they asked in unison, then pushed him into the pool.

He sank to the bottom, then floated there, looking up, the ripples on the surface seeming to take the shape of a woman.

He kicked toward the surface, toward the woman, toward the truth.

But it kept getting farther and farther away. His lungs burned. His muscles ached. He wasn't going to make it. He was going to go down. Drown. Gone.

And then a hand burst through the water and grabbed his

wrist and hauled him up, up, up until he was gasping on the pool deck.

Adele.

"Let me help you," she said. "I'll always be there to help you."

When Jane found him, Dallas had been sitting on the glider on the porch for two hours. It was still dark. And he was wide awake.

He was, he knew, still in shock.

"Dallas?" She came and sat beside him, dressed only in a thin cotton robe. "What's going on? Are you okay?"

"Adele," he said simply. "The Woman is Adele."

He saw her eyes go wide. Saw her tense and swallow. "Are you certain?"

He stood up, needing to move. He'd been on autopilot for the last two hours, pulling his thoughts together. Hell, pulling his proof together.

And now, goddammit, it was all catching up to him. The horror of this insidious truth. The reality that he had lived. The nature of a woman he had once touched intimately.

Bile rose in his throat.

Oh, god. How the hell did he miss it? How could he not see it?

"Dallas, dammit, talk to me."

"The pieces just started falling together. Her obsession with getting close to me. The way she knew about our relationship."

"She's a therapist. She's trained to see below the surface."

"The way she predicted that someone would leak that we had sex when we were in that cell. Who else knows that? Who else has been consistently in our lives?" His voice took on a hard edge. He saw it so damn clearly now, why didn't she?

Now she stood, too, then started pacing. "But it hasn't been consistent. Adele didn't marry Colin until after we were in college. That was years after the kidnapping."

"Plenty of time to set up a new identity. To change her appearance, even. Heal from surgical scars."

Jane licked her lips. "But—" She cut herself off with a frown, not sure how to contradict him.

"You see it, too, don't you?"

"I don't want to. Oh, god, Dallas, I don't want to. But it makes sense."

"It more than makes sense. It's blindingly obvious now that I've backed away. I was too close before. I mean, hell, at one time I even suspected her of writing those damn letters. But I ruled it out."

She nodded. "You told me. But you ruled her out because the timing was off. Not because you didn't think she had it in her to go psycho-stalker on you." She exhaled loudly. "Shit, Dallas. This is—"

"Huge," he said. "A complete mind fuck. Yeah. I know."

She sat on the glider. "The letters started while you were still—"

"Together. Yeah." He felt ill. "The letters were essentially about me not being with whoever was writing them. It didn't make sense for it to be Adele."

"But you were still playing the King of Fuck. A girl can get jealous. Especially a psychotic one. Oh, god, Dallas."

He didn't want it to be true. Hell, it *couldn't* be true. He'd slept with her. He'd done dark, fucked up, wicked things with her.

His knees went weak and he reached for the porch railing.

"Dallas!"

"I'm okay, I'm okay."

"Adele killed that poor dog," Jane said, then looked at him. "Are you sure? Can we prove it?"

"That's what I've been working on for the last two hours."

"And?"

"And so far we know that she flew into Vegas the day before you found the dog in your driveway. She checked into the Bellagio and had appointments at the spa. She returned to the East Coast yesterday morning."

"It's not a hard drive from Vegas to LA," Jane said. "Did she actually go to the spa?"

"Someone using her name did, but I'm betting she paid a show girl to pretend to be her, go have a massage and a facial, and not say a word. Liam's checking that out right now. But what's even more interesting, Noah had to really dig for any information on Adele that's more than five years earlier than the date she married Colin. What he did find has earmarks of being fabricated. He's verifying."

"How?"

"Computer checks, follow-ups. But I'm doing my own verification." He drew in a breath and met her eyes. "I told Quince to ask Colin one very specific question. Was the woman we know as Adele working with him on our kidnapping?"

"You've already asked?"

He nodded, then held up his phone. "I'm expecting an answer any minute. Quince has already said that the Woman may have faked her death. That's why Colin could pass a polygraph saying that she was dead. To him—hell, to her—the woman in the cell with us is dead. A brand-new woman took her place."

"That's bullshit," Jane said.

"Agreed. But it's the kind of trick intelligence officers use to fool polygraphs. We should hear from Quince soon."

They both stared at the phone as if it were a live bomb. And when it rang, Jane actually jumped.

Dallas answered before the first ring finished. "Tell me."

"She's the one. Sorry, mate. I know she was a friend."

Except of course she wasn't. Dallas had only thought she was. Adele had played him in a cell seventeen years ago, and she was playing him still.

Fuck.

Dallas closed his eyes, forcing himself to stay calm. Professional. "No, this is good," he said to Quince. "This is information. Get out to Connecticut and bring her in. Whatever you need to do, I want her in the cell next to Colin."

"You got it," Quince said. "The team's already en route. They wanted to be positioned if we got the answer from Colin we expected."

"Call me back when you have her."

"Will do," Quince said and ended the call. The minute the line went dead, Dallas deflated, every ounce of professional bravado leaving him. He leaned against the porch rail, Jane right beside him, then dragged his fingers through his hair as he tried to process all the shit that just seemed to keep swirling in his mind.

"I slept with that woman. Hell, I did more than just sleep with her. I did things—let her do things—and I had no idea. No idea at all that she'd touched me before. That she'd fucking used me. *Tortured me.*"

How could he not have known?

How could he have missed it?

He kept his hands fisted, not so much in anger, but in an effort to hold in every bit of himself. He was on the verge of unraveling, goddammit, and he wouldn't let her have that, too. He had to keep his shit together or else she won. She fucking won.

"It was dark," Jane said. Her voice was deceptively calm. "She wore a mask. It was years between the kidnapping and her showing up as Colin's wife. And god knows Adele has had plastic surgery. You couldn't have known, Dallas. No one would have even suspected."

"I should have. I've been looking for the bitch for seventeen years. *I* should have suspected."

"*No.*" Her voice was fierce, and when she came over and grabbed his arms, her grip was so tight he thought she might actually bruise him. "Don't you dare pull back on me because of this. Don't you dare let her win."

She sucked in air. "You're going to work through this. We both will. She played games with you, Dallas. With both of us. Psychotic, fucked up games."

Tears streamed down her face, but he didn't think she even knew she was crying. "We're stronger together than apart. We always have been. We know it, and god knows she knew it, too. It's why she tried to destroy us. But it didn't work. It won't ever work."

Her words sang to him, and he wanted to tell her that she was right. That she—that *they*—were what mattered. But the words seemed to get lost in his throat, and he couldn't speak. Hell, his chest was so full of pain and love and grief he could barely breathe.

But she had to know, and so he pulled her close and kissed her, pouring all of his love, all of his fear, all of his need into that touch, that connection. She was right—they *were* better together—and as she melted against him, opening herself to him, he drew her in. Her strength, her ferocity, her love.

"You're everything to me," he said when they broke apart. They were both breathing hard, and he couldn't take his eyes off her. He needed to lay her down and claim her. He craved the sensation of her body pressed against his, giving herself completely to him. Completing him.

"Yes," she said. It was all she said, but it was enough. He pushed her back until her ass was against the railing, and she was holding on to the newel post with her right hand. He threaded the fingers of his left hand in her hair, holding her head in place as he attacked her mouth while he used his left to untie her robe, letting both halves fall open, exposing her breasts, her belly, her sweet pussy.

He slid his hands down, and his cock hardened even more when he found her slick, wet heat. She spread her legs, her free hand on the back of his neck as he pulled her closer, deepening the kiss even as his fingers thrust hard inside her.

Roughly, he pulled her head back then looked into her eyes, so dark with passion. Her lips were swollen from his assault, and she was breathing hard. "Now," she begged. "Fast. Hard. Please."

He didn't hesitate. He was wearing nothing but the loose athletic shorts he'd pulled on before coming outside, and now he pushed them down, stepping out of them and kicking them off to the side. She still wore the robe, and it fluttered in the breeze as he moved closer, then curled one hand around her waist, under the robe so that he felt the heat of her skin against his palm.

She was breathing hard, looking deep into his eyes. "Only you," he said.

"I know. God, Dallas, I've always known."

"Put your legs around me," he ordered, moving closer. He teased the tip of his cock against her pussy as she did, and he was so damned aroused he almost came right then. He held it back, though. He wanted—*needed*—to be inside her.

Slowly he entered her, watching the passion on her face as she tilted her head back. As her nipples peaked and her breathing became more and more shallow. She bit her lower lip and he knew that she was holding back a cry.

He pushed in more, and then more still when her legs tightened around his ass, urging him closer and closer until he was balls-deep inside of her, enveloped in the heaven of her wet heat.

"Make it hard, Dallas. Make me come."

He didn't move a muscle, and she whimpered and squirmed in frustrated protest.

"Do you trust me?"

"You know I do."

He slid his other arm around her waist, so that he was holding her steady with both hands. "Then let go of the post. Drop your legs from around me. Then lean back. Let your arms fall, too."

"Dallas, no—"

"Yes." The command in his voice was inescapable. "I want you to watch the stars, and I want to watch you. And I want to be the only thing keeping you from falling."

"You already are," she said, the deep sincerity in her voice filling his heart even as the heat on her face made his cock throb inside her. Slowly, she let go of the post and then leaned back so that only her ass was on the railing. The rest of her was laid out flat, kept from falling only by his hands on her back, and connected only by the length of his cock inside her.

She was his, all right. As surely as he belonged to her.

The thought filled him. Excited him. And he held tight to her waist as his hips moved, pounding a steady rhythm inside her, one that built in power and intensity as she cried out his name. As she gave herself entirely to him, trusting him to keep her safe as she floated under the wide expanse of stars.

"Dallas!" Her cry rent the night, and at the same time, her body clenched tight around him and she shook from the power of the orgasm that broke through her, giving him that final push into a wild oblivion. With a guttural cry, he exploded, filling her, holding her, loving her.

He pulled her back up to him, craving the feel of her skin against his chest and her mouth against his. She clung to him, her body still trembling as her legs once again wrapped around his hips, keeping them connected, so that there was nothing separating them. They were one in that moment. Whole. Complete. Perfect.

When she finally leaned back, he saw the fire in her eyes. "Wow," she said, and he couldn't help but laugh with her.

"Yeah," he agreed. "Definitely wow."

"So," she said, trailing a fingertip down his chest. "Wanna go inside and go for round two?"

He was still inside her, and though he'd been soft, he felt himself get rock hard again.

She grinned at him. "Yeah," she said. "I guess you do."

With a laugh, he started toward the door, holding her tight against him, but the sharp, familiar ring of his phone made him freeze.

"Liam?" she asked as she slid down his body.

With a nod, he grabbed his phone off the table in front of the glider, then answered the call. "Tell me."

"Her house is empty," Liam said. "But there's no reason to think she knows we suspect her. Looks like she's just gone out of town and a chat with her gardener confirms that."

"In that case," Dallas said, "I think I have a way to draw her back home."

25

Soaring

I am the bait.

I know I'm safe and we're setting a trap and everything is under control, but I'm still nervous. And as our plane starts its descent toward JFK, I take another look at the text conversation on Dallas's phone:

Dallas: You there?

Adele: For you? Always.

Dallas: Need to ask a favor.

Adele: Whatever you need.

Dallas: Jane and I flying back from LA today. It will be crazy with the press after that piece about our kidnapping. I want her out of the limelight.

Adele: I agree, but what can I do?

Dallas: Meet us at the airport? I can take a cab home, but I was thinking you could take her to your house? The press won't look for her there, and she can rest and regroup while this dies down. Just a day or two. Would be a huge help.

Adele: Of course! You two are like my family. Send flight details and
   I'll be there.

Dallas did, of course. And now the plan is that he and I go
back to New York as usual, get our luggage, head outside, and
then when she pulls up to supposedly give me a ride, the team
will swoop in and grab her.

It's risky in such a public place, but the guys have it planned
out in such a way that, if everything goes right, Adele will be
unconscious in seconds and Tony will drive her vehicle away
right under everyone's noses.

Considering covert operations isn't my thing, I'm simply
going to trust them. And cross my fingers very, very tightly.

Mostly, though, I'm going to leave the Adele side to the
guys, because I know that I'm going to be mostly preoccupied
with the crush of reporters and cameras.

And it turns out I'm right.

The madness begins the moment we hit baggage claim at
JFK. Reporters with cameras and microphones get in our faces,
trail us as we walk, and shout out everything from compli-
ments to insults, all with the hopes of making us look in their
direction so that they can get that perfect shot to sell to the
tabloids or go viral on Instagram.

Before—in the pre-disinherited days—we'd have been met
by one of the Sykes conglomerate's security guards who double
as drivers. Usually someone big and burly who would keep the
press away. Better yet, we would have flown in on one of the
family's private jets and avoided the cameras altogether.

To be fair, in the past, I wouldn't have attracted much attention, if any. Wealth and a household name was hardly enough
to maintain tabloid interest in me, and I usually flew under the
radar unless I had a book out or lunch with a celebrity who really was Twitter worthy.

Dallas, of course, has always been a tabloid favorite, but he'd manufactured that persona and encouraged it.

We get our minimal luggage, and I hold tight to Dallas's hand as we keep our heads down and our sunglasses on. As if UV protection is sufficient to allow us to hide in plain sight.

The crowd is rowdy, shifting from simply photographing us to shouting insults, screaming that we're sinners, that it's Dallas's fault that poor dog is dead.

"You'll burn in hell!"

"Whore!"

"Dallas! Dallas! Do you think religious zealots sacrificed that dog?"

"Jane, give us a smile for the camera."

I don't look—I keep my eyes focused on the floor—but when I hear the wail, I can't help but turn my head just quick enough to see a woman tumble to the ground, taking a reed-thin man with a camera down with her.

"Bitch!" the man yells as two burly security guards rush to pull him away before his fist smashes into her face.

They've completely drawn the focus away from us, and for that much at least I'm grateful. Even so, an unwelcome surge of panic rushes through me, and I just want Adele to pull up so that we can get this over with. But she doesn't. And doesn't.

And thirty minutes later she hasn't answered Dallas's texts or shown up.

"Any sign of her?" Dallas asks, talking with Liam on his phone. I lean close so that I can hear what they're saying.

"Nothing. Maybe she—wait. Noah found her. Patching him in."

"Got her," Noah says.

"Where? This terminal."

"Across the goddamn Atlantic. She hopped a plane to London late yesterday. She must have gotten wind of the fact that we were scoping out her house."

"And she just answered my texts from the goddamn UK."

"There's more," Noah says. "Get this, her seat mate was a guy named Christopher Brown. He's from Queens. And he owns a white cargo van."

"They're running," I say.

"Looks like it," Dallas says, and then to Liam and Noah, "I'm getting Jane home. We need to talk to our parents today, but you guys find out everything you can about Brown and see if you can track the two of them in the UK. Give me a few hours and I'll check back in."

I'm tense in the taxi home, not sure if it's good or bad that Adele is gone. I'm happy to have her in another country, but I'd rather have her behind bars. And on top of that, I'm guessing that the press is going to be just as crazy at our apartment, and I'm really not in the mood to deal.

But when we pull up in front of my building, I don't see any signs of paparazzi. I say a silent thank-you to the media gods who are, for once, protecting instead of pelting us with bolts of lightning.

My relief, however, is short lived, because the moment we step into the building, I see Bill waiting in the lobby. Bobby, one of the doormen, stands beside him, managing to look both official and embarrassed.

"Why are you here?" I ask, but it's Bobby who answers.

"He wanted to wait in your apartment, but that just wouldn't do. Not without a search warrant. Even being your ex-husband, Ms. Martin, I couldn't just let him in your apartment."

"No," I say slowly, dread growing inside me. "You couldn't." I focus on Bill, who's standing now. And, I notice, his attention is on Dallas, not me.

"What's going on?" I pray my voice sounds normal.

He shifts his gaze to me, then lifts an eyebrow. "What's going on? Apparently a hell of a lot more than you bothered to tell me when we were married."

My stomach twists as I realize that he learned about both my kidnapping and what happened between Dallas and me in that cell from the tabloids. "Bill, I'm so, so sorry. We—we should talk."

"No," he says harshly, then turns back to face Dallas. "You're the one I need to talk with right now."

26

Mano a Mano

"All right," Dallas said, sitting on the sofa and not bothering to offer Bill a chair. "You want to talk? Let's talk."

Bill glanced toward the bedroom, where Jane had excused herself, but not before shooting Dallas a worried look. He'd simply brushed a kiss over her lips, certain he looked passably nonchalant.

But while he'd had years of practice camouflaging his nerves, that didn't change the fact that right now he *was* worried. What did Bill suspect? More to the point, what could Bill prove?

"I'd rather talk somewhere else. Do you have an office? Is there a common area in the building we can use?"

"It's a one-bedroom apartment, Bill. In case you missed the memo, Jane and I recently saw the tide turn in our fortunes. But have a seat." Now he did gesture to the sofa. All things considered it probably made more sense to at least be cordial to the man. "We can talk here."

"It's just that Jane . . ." He drifted off, glancing toward the closed bedroom door.

"Is that what this is about?" Dallas leaned back, purposely not crossing his arms over his chest. He wanted to look open, not closed off. And most definitely not defensive. "My relationship with Jane?"

"No. Well, yes, in a way. I just don't think that what I have to say is something you want her to overhear."

"Bill, you're trying my patience. Whatever you have to say to me you can say to Jane." No worry here. Nothing to hide at all. "So come on. What's got you so worked up you came all the way up from Washington to see me? Frankly, I don't think there's been a day in your life where I was the man at the top of your list. Except that one time. What was that, again?" He pulled a frown. "Oh, wait, I remember. When you decided to investigate my kidnapping against my wishes."

"I remember that, too," Bill said, still standing. "I wondered why you were so intent on blocking that investigation."

"Oh, I don't know. Maybe because you were fucking around in my life without my permission?"

"Possibly. Or it could be that you were afraid that investigating your kidnapping would lead down all sorts of strange rabbit holes."

Dallas felt his stomach clench and told himself to just keep breathing. "If you're going to talk in riddles, Bill, you're going to have to come up with something cleverer. Or at least clearer."

"You want clarity?" He took two steps forward. If Dallas had been standing, they would have been nose to nose. "How's this? I think you didn't want WORR or the FBI investigating because you were afraid we'd learn about Deliverance. How's that for some fucking clarity?"

"Deliverance?" *Shit, shit, goddamn motherfucking shit.* "You're talking about that vigilante organization that Jane's focusing on in her upcoming book? What the hell does that have to do with me?"

"A lot, I'm thinking. And if you've dragged Jane down into any of your sordid shit, Dallas, I swear to god I'll—"

"*What?*" Dallas was on his feet, because as soon as Bill brought Jane into this, the gloves were off. "What the hell do you think I'm doing? And why the hell would you think I've dragged her anywhere?"

Bill actually laughed. "Are you kidding me? Do you think I haven't checked you out fully? Do you think I don't know who your real father is?"

"You son of a—"

"And then you stoop so low as to seduce your sister . . ."

"You have no idea what we are to each other." He ground out each word, a vile anger bubbling inside him. "No idea how we saved each other."

"I know you poisoned her," Bill countered. "Not physically, maybe, but you destroyed her all the same."

"No," he said. "*No*. I saved her. And whether you understand it or not, she saved me." He strode forward, getting in the other man's face. "She loves me, Bill, and that's what you can't stand. That you never really had her. That she was always mine, even when you called her wife."

Bill blanched, but otherwise didn't falter. "Maybe so. Maybe she doesn't love me. But that's too bad, because she damn sure picked the wrong man. What is she going to do when you're locked away? Because you will be, Dallas. I've been asking questions. Lots of questions. And guess what? I'm starting to find answers, too."

He took a step closer. "Think about that, Dallas." His voice was low. Threatening. "Because I promise you—I damn sure will be."

27

Liar's Game

"You heard all that?"

I've stepped quietly from the bedroom and into the living room to find Dallas standing by the window. He hasn't turned to look at me. He's just standing, frozen, looking toward the roof of the next building over and at the tiny sliver of Central Park we can see in the distance.

I come up behind him and curve my arms around his waist, then rest my head on his back. "He can't prove anything," I say. "He's just guessing. Positioning. It's more about me than about you."

He turns, then kisses me tenderly before leaning back to look into my eyes. "That's true. But he'll be like a dog with a bone on this, because he knows he's right even if he can't prove it. Yet. And he'll keep digging and digging. He won't give up, Jane. He won't give up because of you."

I swallow, suddenly cold, because he's right.

"He'll keep at it until he gets enough proof to arrest me, and once that happens, I'm done. Hell, I'm essentially done now, because he damn sure has me under surveillance."

"Dallas, no." I understand what he's saying—it makes perfect sense—and yet I can't quite process it. This is who Dallas is. *What* he is. And yes, I understand the irony of that thought. Because god knows I believed Deliverance was vile in the beginning. But that was before my eyes were opened, and now I understand what Deliverance does, not to mention how Dallas's role in that mission has shaped the man he's become.

"If he can prove this," Dallas says gravely, "he'll have me in a cage so fast it makes both our heads spin."

I swallow and cling to his arms. He bends forward, then pulls me to him and holds me tight. "After all this," he says, "after everything we've been through, I can't stand the thought that this is what breaks us."

"If it comes to that, we leave," I say recklessly. "We run." I can't bear the thought of being without him, either.

But Dallas only laughs. "Break another rule? Embarrass the family again? Take you away from Lisa forever? From Brody and Liam and Archie? Baby, I said I would protect you always, and I meant it. Even if that means protecting you from my mistakes."

"It won't happen," I say firmly. "I'll talk to Bill. I'll fight. We'll make Daddy hire the best attorneys, and—" I cut myself off on a sob.

"We have to tell them," I say. "About Colin and Adele for sure. Maybe about everything."

Dallas nods. "I know. Even if Adele's flown the coop, we still need to tell Mom and Dad about her. And about Colin. They need to know."

"Dad will feel vindicated," I predict. "But Mom—Dallas, it's going to completely wreck her."

"It will," he agrees, looking as miserable as I feel. "But what choice do we have?" he asks, and I have no answer. Because he is right.

It is time. Time to break our mother's heart.

28

Truth & Consequences

He learned from Archie that his parents were spending the week in their Park Avenue apartment, and he said a silent thank-you that they didn't have to drive all the way to the Hamptons.

Then again, when the taxi pulled up in front of the stately pre-war building, Dallas almost wished they still had a few hours to go. He wasn't ready to dump this truth on his parents. Hell, he doubted he'd ever be ready. From the way Jane was sitting beside him, her fingers twined so tight in his that her knuckles were white, he knew she felt the same.

"Come on," he said. "Let's do this."

Considering the width and breadth of his father's banishment of them, he almost feared that Charlie, the doorman, would turn them away, even though Jane had called from the car to tell Lisa they had something to talk about and were on their way over. But while Dallas was certain the man he'd known for years had pity in his eyes, his professional demeanor never faltered. He rang the apartment to announce them, nodded in confirmation, then called the elevator for them.

He and Jane stepped on together, and the moment the doors closed she lifted herself onto her toes and kissed him. "For luck," she said.

Lisa stood in the foyer when the elevator door opened, her arms wide to draw them both in. She hugged them tight and whispered, "Just give him time. Give him time."

She was talking, of course, about Eli, who stood behind her, his arms crossed over his chest, and a scowl cut deep into his face. "I assume this is about your relationship," Eli said as he led them into the den. "And your inheritance."

"No, sir," Dallas said. He glanced at Jane, who gave him a small smile as if for strength. "It's about Colin. And it's about Adele."

Lisa's eyes darted between the two of them. "Is he dead? Oh, dear god, did something happen to Colin? Adele must be a wreck. She's called almost every day wondering if I've heard from him. I can't say I've ever liked that woman much, but I can tell she's scared to death for him."

"He's missing," Dallas began. "But not in the way you think."

"What do you mean?"

"Bill told us the FBI is after him," Jane said. "We figure the FBI's either found him, someone he crossed found him, or he's on the run."

"What did I say?" Eli commented. "Didn't I tell you he got his hands into something dirty again. What is it? More tax fraud?"

"Kidnapping," Dallas said flatly, as Jane moved to sit by Lisa and take her hand. "Our kidnapping."

"What?" Lisa blinked, confused. "What do you mean your kidnapping?"

"He was behind it, Mom," Jane said gently. "Colin was the man behind our kidnapping."

Across the room, Eli made a noise that was something between a cough and a cry. He looked between all of them, his face turning an almost comic shade of red. Then he picked up a Tiffany vase that must have cost a fortune and hurled it across the room where it shattered on the tile in front of the fireplace.

"Eli!"

But he didn't answer. He didn't do anything except march out of the room, leaving his wife and his children behind.

Lisa started to rise, but Jane tugged her down. "No. You know Daddy. Give him a minute."

Lisa nodded. They all knew Eli. His temper was usually a slow burn, but sometimes it burst out with dragon-like fury. He'd work through it and come back and comfort his wife. Until then, Dallas and Jane would take care of Lisa.

"Are you sure? Maybe there's been a mistake."

Jane caught Dallas's eye, and he saw the unspoken question: how much could they tell her?

"Of course there hasn't been a mistake." Eli's deep voice resonated through the room, and Dallas turned to see his father standing in the doorway. Tall and proud and pissed as hell. "Of course he did it. We should have seen it. We should have known." He crossed the room and sat next to Lisa, then pulled her into his arms, a limp, weary woman compared to his strong, angry resiliency.

"He did it to punish us," Eli continued. "He did it to hurt you. To hurt me. It was never about the children."

"No." She tilted her head up. "No, he would never do that to Jane. Or to Dallas," she added, but from the way she blinked, Dallas could see that she wasn't quite sure. That part of her believed it, and understood. "No," she repeated. "I was his wife. I would know if he was capable of that."

"He's a psychopath," Eli said, stroking her hair. "He knew—knows—how to hide."

"It's worse," Jane said. "We—we think Adele is involved, too. We—we wanted you to know in case she contacts you. Right now she's on the run—we know she's gone to London. But who knows how long she'll stay there, and she may reach out to you. But don't see her, Mom. If she wants to have lunch, come up with an excuse. But whatever you do, don't see her."

For a moment, even Eli was speechless. Dallas got that—it was a hell of a reality to absorb in just moments.

Then Lisa shook her head violently, as if that was the only way to silence the noise inside. Then she stood. "I—I have to go. I need to walk."

"Darling, no." Eli held her hand between his, and Dallas saw so much love and concern in his eyes that for that one moment in time, he forgave his father every wrong. "Stay here. Lie down. I'll make you a drink."

But she pressed her lips together and shook her head. "No, I'm okay, truly. Well, no, I'm not. But I need air. I just want fresh air. I'll only go across the street. But I'm feeling trapped, Eli. I need—"

"I'll walk with you, Mom," Dallas said.

"No." Eli's voice was firm. "Please," he said less forcefully. "Jane can go with her mother. I'd like to speak to you."

Dallas glanced toward Jane, who hooked her arm through Lisa's. "Come on, Mom. Why don't we walk to the park?"

Dallas knew they were tempting the paparazzi, but he could tell Lisa needed to get out, and Jane gave him a nod, letting him know she was up for it. Thankfully, he didn't have to worry about Adele or her cohort. They were an entire ocean away.

Dallas and Eli watched them go, and as they disappeared behind the elevator's doors, Dallas felt some of the weight of the day leave him, too. Yes, he was numb. But at the same time it felt good to tell them at least part of the truth. To give them some closure even if the circumstances were horrible.

There was more to tell, of course. They were still holding tight to the secret about Deliverance. About Bill breathing down his neck. But that was for later. Maybe—if they got lucky with Bill and his band of merry investigators—that discussion could even be tabled indefinitely.

Right now, though, neither Bill nor Deliverance mattered. All Dallas wanted was to hear what his dad had to say. He knew better than to get his hopes up, but he couldn't help the tiny voice that suggested that the only reason his dad would want to see him alone would be to discuss Dallas's proposal about rescinding the adoption.

"This is going to be hard on your mother," Eli said as they moved from the foyer back to the den and sat down.

"Very," Dallas said. "She was married to him for years. She never knew how far he would go."

He understood that. It wasn't the same as his situation with Adele, of course. But close enough that he could empathize with his mother. That he would understand how blind and vulnerable and foolish she was feeling.

"We weren't responsible, your mother and I."

Dallas cocked his head. "I'm sorry?"

"It was good we terminated his rights," Eli continued. "Maybe that set him off—maybe that flipped the switch and made him go after you—but we couldn't have known it would end up that way."

Dallas blinked, not sure if he should feel angry that his father was trying to exonerate himself, or sad that Eli felt so much guilt that he was trying to now dig his way clear. In the end, he just felt sad, and a little exhausted.

"Dad," he said. "Of course you weren't responsible. Neither was I and neither was Jane. Colin's the guilty one."

"Damn right. The man's a lunatic. Who knows what he would have done to Jane if we hadn't filed the termination papers? If our Jane lived part of every year under that monster's roof? Sometimes it's best to end things."

"Yes, sir."

"I've been thinking about you and Jane," he continued, and Dallas felt a glimmer of hope. Surely that meant he'd been thinking about the rescission.

"First of all, I want to put you back on the payroll. Return to some level of normalcy, and move on."

Dallas swallowed, hoping that was possible, but fearing it never would be. Not with Bill out there hunting him.

Still, he spoke the truth when he said, "I'd like that."

"I thought so. I hoped so. And I want you as chief operating officer of either our UK or German division." He paused and looked at Dallas expectantly. "Well? What do you think?"

Dallas frowned, uncertain. "You think Jane and I would be less in the public eye overseas?"

The minute he said the words, he knew that he'd entirely misread the situation.

"Jane would be here, most likely in her house in LA. That's what you two need, Dallas. What this family needs. Time. Distance."

Dallas stood, propelled to his feet by the force of his fury, a rage he just barely kept under control. "How the hell can you not get it? She's the love of my life. We'd already be married if it weren't for the adoption. And time and distance isn't going to change that. Hell, I wouldn't want it to, and neither would she."

"Calm down, boy. You're being—"

"I'm not being anything but honest. You can't just—"

His goddamn phone rang, but since it was Liam, he held up a finger to his dad. "What?" he snapped.

"She doubled back, Dallas. The bitch doubled back after she

landed in London. Do you understand? She's in New York. Adele's somewhere in the city right now."

Liam was still talking as Dallas raced for the service stairs, not willing to wait for the elevator. He was breathless when he burst into the lobby after running down eight flights, but he didn't stop.

He hurled himself toward the door, only to find Charlie hurrying toward him with almost as much speed.

"Where are they?"

"There was a van." Charlie gulped in air. "A van hit your mother in the intersection. She's still there. I've called 911 and a doctor on the sidewalk rushed to help."

"*Jane,*" he demanded. "What about Jane?"

Charlie's eyes went wide. "Gone! A man got out of the van and grabbed her, and then drove away. I didn't know what to do. I told the 911 dispatcher and cops are coming, too, and I—"

But though he kept on talking, Dallas didn't hear a word. His head was too full of rage, and his heart was too full of fear.

29

Bitch Is Back

My head is pounding when I wake, and though I try to open my eyes, I can only manage to squint. Dozens of spotlights are aimed right at me, and I can see nothing except pure white light and faint spectral arcs in my periphery that seem to be dancing and leaping.

I'm dizzy, and I remember being stabbed with a needle. Some sort of hallucinogen, I think, considering the way the world seems to be all wonky.

A moment later, I realize that I'm standing. I try to raise my hand to shield my vision, but it's impossible. My wrists are strapped behind me, and my back is pressed to a pole. I try to step forward, but there are ties on my ankles as well as one around my waist.

It's the one that encircles my neck that terrifies me the most.

I don't know where I am, but I do know who brought me here. And that certainty makes my blood run cold.

"Adele," I say, though the name is only a whisper. "Please. My mom. Where's my mom?"

I don't really expect an answer. I know how she works. She will leave me here for hours upon hours. Sweat pouring down me from the heat of these lamps. My mouth dry with the need of water. My muscles aching and trembling. My stomach clenching, and my head woozy from fear and hunger. She will push me to the edge, and when I am close to tumbling over into insanity or death, she will bring water. Bread. Maybe boiled meat.

And then the horror will start up again.

Or maybe not. Maybe this time she's tired of her games. Maybe this time she just wants to kill me.

What was it her text message said? That she could have done so much worse?

This, I think, is worse.

"Adele, please . . ."

And then I hear her heels. Those damned stilettos she always wears. They click across the concrete floor, and if I squint I can barely make out her movement to my left. She steps to one side so that she is blocking one of the spotlights.

Now I can see her silhouette against the light. I can't make out her face, but I'm sure that she is smiling, simpering and cold and crazy.

"Please what? Please make this fast? I don't want to make it fast. You've made me suffer for seventeen years. I don't think you'll be able to hold on for that long, but I'm willing to try if you are."

"I thought we were friends, Adele," I say. Not because I believe it but because I am desperate. "Why are you doing this?"

"Darling, we *are* friends. Or I thought we were, too. You stayed away from him, just like a friend should stay away from another woman's man. I don't hold a grudge about what you did when you were young—teenagers can do such foolish things—but once you grew up, you understood. You left. And, Janie darling, you were right. You even got married, you totally cleared the path. And then," she says, the soft edge of her voice turning as sharp as a blade, "then you twisted it all around.

"You want to know why I'm doing this? I'm doing it because *you* started it. Because you left me no choice. Because when someone tries to take what is yours, the only option left is to fight. And, darling Janie, this is a fight I promise you I'll win."

I wish I could see her face. I want to see the crazy in her eyes. I want to face down the monster who's been haunting us all this time.

But all I can do is talk to the shadow.

All I can do is pray that Dallas finds me in time.

Because I don't need to see her face to know that if she has her way, I'm not getting out of this room alive.

30

Tick Tock

"Goddammit, we're running out of time," Dallas bellowed as he burst through the door and into Deliverance's headquarters.

Thirty-seven fucking minutes had already passed—thirty-seven minutes since a white van took down his mother in the intersection, and most likely would have killed her had Jane not been there to pull her enough out of the way to lessen the blow. Thirty-seven minutes since a man with a full beard and dark glasses leaped from the passenger side door and dragged Jane away from Lisa's side. Thirty-seven minutes since the man slammed the door shut, trapping Jane inside as the unseen driver sped away, leaving Lisa bleeding in the street.

Thirty-seven goddamn minutes since he'd lost her. And that was thirty-six minutes and fifty-nine seconds too long as far as Jane's safety was concerned.

"I know," Liam snapped as he looked up from where he stood in front of a monitor. "Don't you think I know?"

"Sorry—I'm sorry." He knew Liam was just as on edge as he was. Just as worried.

Just as fucking terrified.

"Adele will kill her this time, Liam. Our only chance is to find them fast, and hope she didn't already do it and dump the body."

Christ, were those words even coming out of his mouth?

"We're working on it. We've confirmed that Christopher Brown was one of her patients."

"Tell me about him."

"Christopher Brown, Caucasian male, now twenty-seven. Former juvenile offender. History of sexual abuse, both as a victim and a perp. As an adult, his sheet's long and varied. Arrests ranging from assault, domestic violence, burglary, armed robbery. Pled out for attempted rape, and as part of the deal he agreed to undergo counseling."

"Which is how he met Adele."

"Bingo."

"His residence?"

"That's the question. He rents a house in Queens, but he's not there, and neither are Jane and Adele. Noah and Tony found a receipt for a recent storage shed rental, though. They're en route. I'm expecting them to report back any minute."

Dallas nodded, his gut twisting. "They won't be there. Adele will have her someplace more secure. More private. Too many people coming and going at a storage shed."

He didn't say that the only way they'd find Jane in a storage unit was if that was where Adele had dumped the body. He didn't say it because he couldn't even bear to think it.

"What about property in Adele's name. Still no hits?"

"Nada."

"Shit." He was just about to insist that Liam call Tony and check in when Liam's phone chirped with an incoming text. *Site clear. No J. No A. No sign of recent activity. Dead end. Heading to Breakers.*

"What's that?" Dallas asked, reading over Liam's shoulder.

"A bar Brown is known to hang out in." He sighed, sounding about as miserable as Dallas felt. "We're scraping the bottom of the barrel here, Dallas. The guys are going to ask around. Maybe see if Brown said something. If he mentioned a woman he was seeing, a property he went to with her. Anything that might point us in the right direction."

"We don't have time for that."

"You think I don't know that?" Liam's retort snapped out fast and hard. "*Shit*. Sorry, man. I didn't mean—"

"I know. I get it. *Fuck*. Traffic cams? ATMs? Can we track the van's path? Find out what neighborhood it ended up in?"

"Quince is on it." He pointed to the conference room where Dallas could see Quince pacing behind the glass, a headphone strapped on and a tablet computer in his hand. "He's called in favors with MI6 and also with some friends at the FBI. Nothing yet, but there's a lot of data to sift through. We might get lucky."

"We don't have time for luck. We've only got one chance of finding out where Adele took her. Colin."

Liam shook his head. "We can try again, but he's resistant to the drugs. The only clear results Quince has managed to get have been the polygraph, and it's not like we can point to every building in Manhattan and ask if Adele is there."

"Quince isn't the one going in," Dallas said as Archie approached with mugs of coffee for both men. "I am. And I don't want him drugged. I want him to talk to me."

"You really think he'll tell you anything?"

"He loves Jane," Dallas said simply, then looked at Archie. "You've been there our whole lives. You knew Colin before I ever met him. You saw him with Jane, with Mom. Am I right? Will he tell me?"

Archie's face grew tight. "He's not the man I once knew. But if any hint of that man still exists inside him—yes. That Colin loved his daughter. If he helps you, it will be for her."

"That settles it," Dallas said, and without waiting for either man to respond, he crossed the room to Colin's cell and punched in the code.

"Dallas." Colin looked up as he walked in. His face was drawn, his eyes bloodshot with dark circles that gave him a skeletal appearance. He hadn't shaved in days, and his patchy beard gave him an even more haggard appearance. He sat behind the table, but this time his hands were cuffed to the arms of the metal chair.

He looked defeated.

Dallas hoped to hell he was.

"We know about Adele. You tried to protect her because you love her. I get that. You've been together for even longer than I realized—more than seventeen years. There's a history. There's understanding. But despite all of that, there's your daughter."

While Dallas spoke, Colin didn't move. Hell, he barely breathed. But Dallas saw his eyes flicker just a little at the mention of Jane.

"Adele has her now. She used a van to run Lisa down in the street." Another flicker. And the knuckles on Colin's hands turned white. "When Jane went to help her mother, a man got out of the van and dragged Jane inside." He deliberately didn't say "*our*" mother.

Colin lifted his head. "Where is Adele now?"

And that was it. He had him.

Dallas sat across the table from him. "We don't know. But what I do know is that she'll kill Jane." His voice cracked as he spoke, but he made no effort to hide it. Let Colin see how scared he was. Let him know that the risk to Jane was real. Too damn real.

"I don't understand." Colin's voice was almost a whine. "Why are you in here? Why aren't you out looking for my little girl? What do you want with me?"

"Where are they, Colin?"

"I—I don't know. How could I know?"

Dallas sat back in his chair, trying to give the appearance of a man with all the time in the world. A calm man negotiating a business deal, just like on any other day. "I understand why you didn't tell us earlier that Adele was involved in the kidnapping," he said. "But we know the truth. But we're not upset, Colin. You loved Adele. You were trying to help her."

He leaned forward, then, his eyes tight on Colin's face. "And now I need you to help Jane. Because she needs you desperately. *You're* her father. The man who shares her blood. And you're the only one who can save her. So tell me, Colin. Where would Adele take Jane? Where would she take a woman she wants to torture? To kill."

Colin's shoulders jerked, and he shook his head. "No. No, she wouldn't."

Dallas grabbed the edge of the table, squeezing as tight as he could in an effort to stay calm. To not leap across the table and strangle the man. This stupid, psychopathic lunatic with absolutely no perception of reality. "Do you really think that Adele will let her go? You know the woman better than anyone, Colin. Do you truly believe she'll let Jane live? After what she did to me? After how obsessed she is about me?"

Just saying the words aloud hurt, the effort of forcing them out so intense his entire body ached. He was wound so tight he didn't know how much longer he could hold it in, and he stood up, circling the table and then pacing in front of Colin, hoping the act of moving would help him control his rage.

For Jane, he thought. He had to keep it together for Jane.

Colin just shook his head. "I don't know," he said, a high note of hysteria tainting his voice. "I don't know what you're talking about. What did she do to you? She's your friend, she always has been. And I—I know you two had a relationship, but she's moved on. You've moved on. I don't know what you're talking about."

"You *fucking* liar," Dallas said, his fist swinging out to connect with Colin's jaw.

Violent sobs wracked the older man. "I don't know!" he said. "I don't know what you mean!"

And, goddammit, Dallas believed him. The fear in his eyes. The unfocused terror. Not that he would be discovered lying, but that he would be punished again for something he didn't even understand.

"You worthless bastard," Dallas said. "You planned the kidnapping—don't even try to lie, Quince has done the polygraph, and Ortega suggested as much before he died. Before *you* arranged to have him killed. Now, goddammit, help me find Jane."

"I snapped." Colin choked out the words. "What Eli did. Lisa, how she hurt me. And the money. So broke, and I needed to—"

"You let that bitch have free rein," Dallas growled, interrupting the string of almost incomprehensible excuses.

"No—no. Just food. Water. She took care of you."

Dallas barked out a raucous laugh. "The hell she did." He moved in, then jerked Colin's chair to the side so that he could lean in close, his hands on the arms just above Colin's wrists. "She tied Jane up. Left her in the dark, bound to a table. No food, no water. For hours at a time. Sometimes days."

Colin only whimpered and shook his head.

"But she actually went easy on Jane. It was me she wanted. Me she wanted to break. Maybe she was playing with me because she knew you couldn't give a shit. That you were happy to kill me if Eli didn't pay your fucking ransom. Or maybe she was already obsessed with me. Maybe that's why she snapped so hard—why she's carried this obsession with her for so long. I don't know. I don't fucking care. All I know is that she did things—"

His voice broke, and he took a hard breath as if gathering strength.

"Horrible, sexual things. Emotional things. Sex and mind games and everything in between. She broke me, Colin. She fucking broke me. And Jane is the one who saved me.

"Now that bitch girlfriend of yours has taken Jane. She's going to kill her. Somewhere in that fucked-up brain of hers she thinks that will clear a path to me. Or maybe she knows that I would never be with her, and she's going to kill Jane to punish us both. I don't know. I don't fucking care. All I know is that the woman I love—the woman you fathered and claim to love, too—is going to die if we don't move now. And right now, it's all on you."

"I didn't know! I swear, I didn't know! Oh, god, Dallas, I swear I didn't know!"

Dallas didn't know if he was lying, and right then he couldn't care less. "Then help me, dammit. Tell me where she took her. Tell me before she kills Jane."

For a moment, Colin was silent except for the sound of his ragged, wet breaths. Then he lifted his face and Dallas saw renewed determination. "No."

Dallas reeled backward, the force of Colin's words as powerful as a punch in the gut. "What the hell did you say?"

"No," Colin repeated, and some of his old confidence seemed to flow back into his face. "I have a good idea where Adele would take her. And I'll tell you," he said. "But there's a price."

31

Hide & Seek

Dallas sat beside Liam in the Range Rover as Quince tore through traffic toward the Connecticut farmhouse that Colin had directed them to. A property in need of restoration that Adele had purchased under her true, legal name upon first moving to the States after the kidnapping.

"She said it represented her," Colin had said. "That as she grew and changed, the house would, too. She's like that. Very self-aware. That's why she's such a good therapist. That's why she was able to help me deal with what we'd done—why she urged me to reestablish our relationship when you and Jane were in college."

You fucking idiot, Dallas had wanted to say. Because Colin seemed to truly believe his bullshit. That Adele was some kind of psychological guru, forging a path through both their neuroses. He had no inkling that she was a psychopath, no hint that his own descent had fueled her obsession.

Maybe Colin really was a man who'd spun out of control,

pushed over the edge by the loss of his daughter and financial devastation.

Maybe.

But Adele was just one-hundred-percent fucked up.

And that fact terrified Dallas.

Now, Colin was in the back of the SUV with Noah and Tony on either side of him. He was gagged and wore noise-blocking headphones tuned to classical music, so as to ensure that the men could speak freely without giving Colin any information they didn't want him to have. Dallas didn't truly believe that Colin's reveal of the location was part of a larger plan forged by Adele, but he wasn't taking any chances.

Liam turned to him. "And when it's over? What are we doing with him?"

Dallas's gut clenched. If he didn't need Colin's information, right then he could happily put a bullet through the bastard's brain. Or maybe he couldn't. Though he hated the pity that had welled up inside him, he couldn't deny that he felt it. And that pity just might save the son of a bitch's life.

"We'll worry about that after we get Jane safely out," Dallas said. He shifted in his seat to look back at the man. "And if we don't get her out, then I don't give a shit what happens to him."

The secluded farmhouse stood at the end of a dirt road that opened onto twelve acres of untended apple orchards, and even with Quince behind the wheel it took an hour and a half to get there. When they finally approached the turnoff to the property, Dallas was about to lose his shit.

"We walk from here," Liam said, and Dallas nodded. Right now, Liam was the de facto leader. Not only was Dallas not typically in the field, but he knew damn well his judgment was tainted by fear. "Tony and Noah, get to the house and get the device set up. Stay low, stay quiet. Once you've located them inside, signal us. Colin is going in with me and Dallas. Quince will provide backup from another access point. Tony, you handle anyone else who might be inside the property. Noah, you're on coms unless Quince or Tony need assistance."

They'd already gone over the plan multiple times, but it helped to hear it again. Solidified it. And gave Dallas a sense that this was really going to happen. That they were on it. That they would get in, and get her out.

Back in Manhattan, they'd pulled the farmhouse's original blueprint, but there was no way to know if alterations had been made in the meantime. Hopefully not. Right now, the plan was for Quince and Liam to enter through the cellar access while Colin and Dallas entered through the kitchen door. They'd locate and approach, then assess the situation. If necessary, they'd try to reason with Adele, with Dallas promising her whatever she wanted. But the real mission objective was to take her down, and the men intended to stay hidden long enough to do that, so long as it didn't compromise Jane's safety.

As for Noah's and Tony's assignments, Noah would be stationed near the front door, and Tony would make his own determination once they were aware of how many people were in the property.

That little task was going to be accomplished using the listening device Noah had invented. Though designed for much larger buildings, it should work as well for the house, pinpointing—and relaying—internal conversations. The team anticipated that Jane was being held in either the basement or the attic. By using the device, they could confirm that and conserve valuable time.

Now that they were moving, Dallas removed Colin's headphones, since he'd need to hear and follow instructions. He kept the gag. His tentative trust only stretched so far, and no way was he risking Colin shouting a warning to Adele.

About a hundred yards from the house, Dallas's earpiece

crackled, followed by Noah's voice. "Looks like we've got three in the building. Target is in the basement along with Jane. A male identified as Christopher is on the first floor, kitchen area. Adele spoke to him through the house intercom."

"Jane is okay?" Dallas asked at the same time that Liam asked if there were others inside.

"Can't confirm as to Jane, but best guess is that she's alive and conscious. Adele was talking to her, and the lack of a reply is most likely because of a gag. As for others, it's a possibility. The device detects conversation, not human heat signatures. Could be other targets in the building who are off shift and sleeping, but there's no way to know for sure."

"We haven't had any indication she's working with anyone else," Liam said after they broke the transmission. "But we won't know until we're inside."

Dallas turned to Colin and yanked his gag down. The older man sucked in air, bending over and resting his hands on his knees as he gulped. "Talk," Dallas ordered.

"There won't be anyone else," Colin said softly. He lifted his head and looked between Liam and Dallas. "Adele doesn't trust easily."

"Who's Christopher?"

"A patient. I knew she'd started sleeping with him—I didn't get why." He drew in a breath. "Now, I guess I do."

Dallas looked at Liam. "She knew she needed help."

"Was she sleeping with anyone else?" Liam asked Colin.

"I don't think so."

"Probably just the three of them in there," Liam said, his attention back on Dallas. "Game on."

Liam broke off, following the path Quince had taken, while Dallas and Colin headed for the door. Dallas had a Glock at his waist and a Ruger in his pocket, and he'd happily use either on Adele if she'd harmed even a hair on Jane's head.

"Footsteps." Noah's voice played in his ear as they entered through the kitchen door. "Location indeterminate. I can pinpoint voices with more accuracy."

Dallas said nothing, unwilling to speak and reveal themselves to Adele.

He pointed to the door that led to the cellar. They approached carefully, then opened the door, pistols drawn.

Slowly, they went down the stairs, but the second they reached the concrete floor, Dallas realized that all their planning was for naught.

"Hello, sweetheart," Adele said, her weapon pointed at Jane, gagged and tied to a post. Her eyes were wide, though, and he didn't need words to know that she was terrified. He tried to reassure her, but goddamned if the situation wasn't fucked. He knew Noah could hear everything, but he and Tony would only come if Christopher Brown was taken care of. And what could they do when they arrived, anyway? With a gun at Jane's head, Adele held all the cards.

Especially since Liam and Quince didn't seem to be in the cellar yet.

"Be a good boy and slide your gun over here. Go on," she said. "Do it."

Carefully, he put his Glock on the floor and kicked it toward her.

"Any more weapons on you?" she asked, turning the gun on him as she walked toward him. But it wasn't him she was asking—it was Colin.

"Right front pocket."

"Take it out, darling. Same story. On the ground. Kick it to me." She laughed, then, obviously seeing something in Colin's face. "Well, how do I know what you've been up to? You've been with them. That means you might not be with me anymore."

"Adele," Colin said, as he took the gun from Dallas's pocket, "no."

"You rock solid bastard," Dallas said, though in truth he hadn't expected anything more from the man.

Colin shrugged, then kicked the gun to Adele. "I'm not going to prison, Dallas. Not again."

He looked at Adele. "There are more coming."

She wiggled her fingers at him. "Come join me."

He did, and she turned her gun back on Jane as he approached.

"Insurance," she said, "in case they get in too easily. But I don't think so. I had the cellar door reinforced, and there's no other way in except the way you came. And in case you missed it, that door at the bottom of the stairs we came through? Solid steel. It will take your friends a while to get through."

"You'll never get out," Dallas said.

"Of course we will." She smiled sweetly. "We'll have hostages."

"You miserable bitch." His mind was churning, trying to figure the best plan. If the entrances were reinforced, he needed to buy time so the others could get in. Keep talking and keep her busy. Relay whatever information he could to Noah's headset.

And get her to aim the damn gun somewhere other than at Jane.

"You've disarmed me, Adele. Put your gun down. Let's not risk an accident, okay? There's no reason to keep a gun on her."

"Oh, I think there is."

Dallas kept his eyes on Adele, but he glanced once toward Jane. She stood stoic, her eyes a little unfocused—probably drugged—but she turned to him and he saw the trust there.

Trust he damn sure didn't intend to squander. But right then, he didn't know what the fuck to do next.

"I'm so sorry, Janie," Colin said from where he stood at Adele's side. "I never wanted to hurt you. I just needed the money. Lots of money, and I needed it fast. And I was so angry with Eli and your mother that it seemed like the perfect plan. I didn't know you would be there—I didn't! I just wanted the ransom and then I was going to let Dallas go. But it all spun out of control. Can you forgive me? Please say that you can forgive me."

32

Man Down

I'm so sorry, Janie, I never wanted to hurt you.

Can you forgive me? Please say that you can forgive me.

But how do you forgive someone who so cavalierly stole a chunk of your life?

I don't know, and Colin's words are still echoing in my mind when Adele laughs. "Good god, Colin, could you be more of a sentimental fool?" She waves her gun that is pointed at me, as casually as if she's intending to swat a fly.

I didn't think I had room to be more scared, but my heart starts beating triple-time, the pounding in my ears so loud I'm having trouble hearing her.

"She won't forgive you," Adele says. "Why would she? And why do you need her around when you have me? For that matter, why do I need her around when I have Dallas? He's obsessed with her, you know. And it's always best to break the ties to an obsession quickly, just like ripping off a bandage."

Her words hit my mind in sharp focus, everything hyperreal, and I wonder if that's what it's like for everyone before they die, because she is surely about to kill me, or if it's just the effect of whatever drugs she keeps injecting me with every few hours. Drugs that make my head spin and the world tilt sideways. Drugs that are probably slowly killing me, with just as much certainty as the bullet in that gun.

I squeeze my eyes tight and force my thoughts not to ramble, although why it matters I don't know. I'm gagged, so even if I see some brilliant escape plan, I can't communicate it. All I can do is stand here tied to this post, and bear silent witness to my own demise.

Dallas is to my right, and despite all his promises to protect me, I don't know how that's possible. Even if Adele hadn't taken his gun, he couldn't shoot. Not with her pistol aimed straight at me and her finger on the trigger.

He might not be tied up, but right now, he's as helpless as I am.

And over to my left, I see Quince and Liam creep into the shadows at the far side of the room. I'm guessing they came in through the cellar door, and the reason they're so late is that they either had to get through that asshole Christopher, or Adele's reinforcements to that entrance were solid.

I don't think Adele knows they're there. I can't tell if Colin does, but if so, then that gives me hope, because he hasn't ratted them out. I assume Quince is a good shot, because I always think of him as James Bond. With Liam, I have a little more concrete information, as I know he's an excellent marksman, and almost went to sniper school before shifting gears toward military intelligence.

I've trained with a handgun enough to know that it doesn't much matter. Colin is between them and Adele, and they have no clean shot to either her head or her hand, to blow away the gun. More than that, both those shots are risky and require a buttload of skill. Miss, and Adele takes the next shot, and I'm dead.

For the first time, I'm grateful that Adele has been pumping me full of drugs. Without them, I think I'd be truly freaking out right about now.

"It's time to say goodbye to her, Colin," Adele says, and I realize that I was totally wrong about that freaking out thing. Because now that she's looking at me over the barrel of her gun, I am drowning in ice-cold fear. "Janie, you know I adore you. It's not personal. You're simply an obstacle. And when you're dead, none of this will matter. Not even Dallas."

And then her finger twitches and Dallas howls and lunges forward and I'm sure that it's all over, because he's too damn far away to save me. And I close my eyes and then my ears are screaming because the gun has gone off and now everything sounds hollow and far away, but it's not the sound of death. It's just the sound of gunfire, hard against my eardrums.

Scared, relieved, confused, I open my eyes, only to see a furious Adele whipping around to aim at Colin. In an instant, I realize that he rammed her gun arm, knocking off her aim. And in the process, saving my life.

She's furious, and instead of regrouping and shooting me, she's turning that fury on Colin.

She fires, and he falls, a bright red stain growing on his shirt.

I try to scream, but the gag makes it impossible, and I'm completely incapable of doing anything as Adele turns the gun once again toward me.

But this time Dallas is close, and he leaps the final distance, risking her turning the gun on him.

She does, but not fast enough. He tackles her low, sending her tumbling, and as they go down, Liam and Quince race toward them. And even though Adele recovers quickly, moving to turn her weapon on Dallas, it's too late. Liam kicks her arm and sends the gun flying before she's found her aim, and Quince drops down, presses the muzzle to her temple, and says, very low and very slowly, "Bitch, don't you fucking move."

While Liam and Quince take care of restraining Adele and getting her out of the room, Dallas rushes to me. He uses a knife to unlash me from the post, then rips the gag off me.

He pulls me close, his eyes wet with tears, his expression anguished. "Thank god," he repeats again and again. "Thank god."

I'm sobbing openly now, clinging to him, all of the emotion of the last day pouring out of me like Niagara Falls. "You came," I say. "You came."

He pulls back to look at me. "Of course," he says, and then kisses me hard.

"Is he dead?" I ask when he pulls away.

"He's dead," Dallas confirms.

I turn my head to look at Colin's body. The man who tormented me. The man who saved me. The man who didn't figure out how to be a father until the very end.

I turn back to Dallas, then draw a deep breath. "It's over," I say as he pulls me close once more, his embrace trembling with emotion. "It's really, finally over."

33

Everything Old
Is New Again

Dallas sat on the edge of Jane's hospital bed, stroking her hair.

"I knew you'd rescue me." A weak smile flickered on her lips. "You'll always protect me, right?"

"Always." He closed his eyes and drew in a breath. "God, Jane, I was so afraid I was going to lose you."

"Me, too." She squeezed his hand, her grip weak. "He came through at the end, didn't he?"

"He loved you. He was a complete asshole, and I won't ever forgive him. But at least we know that he loved you."

A tear spilled from her eye. "I'm sad he's dead. Even after everything he did, I'm still sad." She glanced at her IV. "When can I leave?"

"Tomorrow morning. They want to make sure the drug she injected you with is completely out of your system. And let you rest."

"I'm good with the resting part. I'm so tired." She reached for his hand, then squeezed it. "But I'm ready to be home with you."

"I know, baby. Me, too."

"And Mom's doing okay?"

He looked away. Just a split second before his gaze returned to her face, but she noticed.

"What?" she demanded.

"It's not good. They didn't want to worry you when you were first admitted, but she's still unconscious."

She shifted in the bed, as if to rise. "I need to go see her."

"Jane, no. They want you to stay in bed. But I'll go. I'll tell her you're awake and that you say she has to recover. Okay?"

She nodded, her lips pressed tight together in an effort not to cry.

He bent over and kissed her forehead, trying not to cry himself. From worry about his mother. From relief about Jane. "I love you. I'll be back soon. Try to sleep some more."

She nodded, but didn't close her eyes. When he turned back at the door, though, he saw how heavy her lids were.

He blew her a kiss and slid out the door—and found himself face-to-face with Bill.

"Fuck," he said.

"Hello to you, too."

"I promised her I'd go see our mother," he said. "Will you at least give me an hour to do that before you haul me away?"

"I overheard you, and yes."

Dallas drew in a breath, Bill's words as bracing as ice-cold water. One hour of freedom. One hour before he had to tell Jane about the deal he'd cut. One hour before he was back in a cell. Hell, his cell would probably be adjacent to Adele's, who'd been taken away in the chaotic aftermath of the takedown.

"You can have an hour," Bill said, his voice bitter. "Apparently, you can even have forever."

Dallas froze. "What the hell are you talking about?"

"I got a call from a director at MI6 an hour ago. From what

he tells me, Deliverance has been working with that organization for years now."

"That's true," Dallas said, unsure where Bill was going with this and how much he knew. The fact was that Quince hadn't wanted to leave MI6. So he'd worked out a deal with his agency. Only one man there knew about that deal, though, so the fact that Bill was now in the loop was more than a little odd.

"Yeah, well, that director is your goddamn guardian angel, because now the State Department is prohibiting any move to arrest—or even publicly acknowledge—Deliverance or its members. The word is that such an action would be very bad for relations between the US and the UK."

"Really?" Dallas tried not to smile, but it was damn hard to stay stoic. "And you're not going to push the point?"

"I have a lot of friends on the Hill. A lot of powerful connections in the intelligence community and in various Senate oversight committees."

A hint of worry ate at Dallas's good mood. "And?"

"And I thought about it," Bill said. "Then I ruled it out."

"Why?" Dallas asked, then immediately regretted the question. Better to just take the good news and run with it.

Bill had been standing ramrod straight, but now he slouched a little and shoved his hands into his pockets. "To be honest, Dallas, I'm not sure I know. Maybe it's because Deliverance has rescued more than its share of victims. Maybe it's because MI6 values the organization. Maybe it's because I'm just not up for a fight."

He drew a deep breath. "Or maybe it's because I love Jane, and she loves you. More than that, she needs you."

It was the last thing in the world Dallas expected Bill to say. "You're giving Deliverance a pass because of a woman?"

For the first time, Bill's smile seemed more than just polite. "No, I'm giving Deliverance a pass because the State Department told me to. But I'm not fighting that edict because of a woman. And don't look surprised, Dallas. You and I both know that you'd do exactly the same."

"For Jane? Yeah. I'd do whatever it takes."

"I know," Bill said, and Dallas thought that maybe the guy who had once been Jane's husband wasn't a complete dick.

He held out his hand. "Thanks, Bill."

Bill took it, his grip strong. "I'm going to go see Jane for a minute, okay?"

"Sure," Dallas said, with only the slightest hint of lingering jealousy. "She'd like that." And with that strange detente lingering in the air between them, Bill went into the room, and Dallas took off down the hall to check on Lisa.

Since she was in ICU, it took him about ten minutes to get there, and when he walked through her door, his relief at finally arriving immediately evaporated. His father was standing right there. Frankly, Dallas really wasn't in the mood.

He considered leaving, but his father turned, and his expression so mirrored every bit of fear and helplessness that had ripped through Dallas when he'd been terrified of losing Jane, that he couldn't walk away.

"No change," his father said. "I keep telling her to come back, but there's just no change."

Dallas drew closer, then stood at his father's side, his hand on Eli's shoulder. "She's strong, Dad. Give her time. She's in there. She's trying to heal."

He hoped he was right—god, how he hoped he was right. But while he was trying to stay optimistic for his father, the doctors hadn't been able to give them much hope. She was alive, yes, but she hadn't regained consciousness, and if she didn't come around by morning, they were going to put her into a medically induced coma.

They said all the right words about how her vitals looked good and her labs looked good, and yet they couldn't promise that it would turn out okay, and that deep hole of uncertainty terrified Dallas as much as it broke his heart.

"You should try to get some sleep, Dad."

"I can't go home. I can't leave her."

"I know. I get that. I can ask the nurse if they can bring in a cot." Because they were in ICU, Lisa wasn't in a full-blown room with amenities. Just a small, glassed-in area lined with privacy curtains. "If they can't, maybe I can find something for you."

Eli's brow furrowed, and then he turned to Dallas. "Thank you, son."

A lump formed in Dallas's throat, and he tried to swallow it. "Listen, Dad, about everything. We're not going to agree, I know that. But—well, what I said before. About us both wishing I wasn't your son. You know I didn't—"

"My brother was a complete fuckup," Eli said, his harsh interruption so surprising that Dallas simply stared. "Totally useless. You know it. And I know it. And although you may have his blood, Dallas, that's not who you are."

He turned a bit so that he was facing Dallas directly, and there was something on his face that Dallas wasn't sure he recognized. Something he thought just might be respect.

"What you've survived. The man you've become. I watched the way you ran your personal life—a different woman in your bed each night. I kept expecting you to crash and burn. Drugs. Women. Money. Frivolity. All of it. Too much of it."

Dallas had no idea where his father was going with this, but he stayed quiet. Waiting. Hopeful.

"I told you at your great-grandfather's birthday party that I was proud of you, and I meant it. And even later—when all the shit hit the fan with you and your sister—you never let your personal life spill over onto the business. You never truly went off the rails, and god knows you had reason to."

He shook his head as if in disbelief. "Everything you went

through as a young man. Who could have blamed you if you'd turned to drugs? Alcohol?"

"I have my share of issues," Dallas said. "For that matter, so does Jane."

Eli nodded. "I know. And I know I didn't help. That I didn't handle it well afterward. Frankly, it's a testament to your strength of character that you became the man you are."

"Thank you," Dallas said, and he meant it. But he still wasn't sure where his father was going with this. And all he could do was pray that somewhere at the end of this speech, his father was going to tell Dallas that he'd changed his mind. That he was going to rescind the adoption.

"And I'm proud that you're my son," Eli continued, and with the inclusion of that one little word, hope faded. "Because you *are* my son. And Jane is my daughter. And nothing will ever change that."

And there it was. The light snuffed out. Hope killed.

His family destroyed. Because Dallas wasn't going to sacrifice his and Jane's love at the altar of their father's pride. He'd hire his own attorneys. He'd fight the battle, but even though he was now an adult, without Eli's consent, the odds of the judge rescinding the adoption were slim. There just wasn't much precedent, and courts were loath to interfere with family relationships unless there was full consent on all sides.

And even if he won, the victory would be hollow by its very nature. Because whatever threads of family still remained would be completely and finally destroyed.

At the thought, Dallas's heart constricted. He wanted to shake Eli, to make him understand. He wanted to fight, dammit. But how did he fight perception and pride? How did he open his father's eyes?

Dallas drew a deep breath and hoped that when he spoke his voice wouldn't be stained by anger and disappointment.

"I'm happy I'm not a disappointment to you, sir," he said. "But maybe we'd all be better off if I was."

Eli's brows rose, and then, unexpectedly, he burst out laughing. "Why? Because then I'd want to get rid of you? Not only cut you off financially, but trim your branch from the family tree?"

"Well, actually, yes." Dallas frowned. Why the hell was that funny?

"You think I don't understand how you feel about Jane, and maybe you were right. Back then. But you're not right anymore." He glanced toward Lisa, his chest rising and falling with a deep sigh. "I know what it's like to love someone. And I'm terrified that I'm going to know soon what it's like to lose them."

He shifted, turning his face away as he roughly wiped his eyes. "I don't want my children to feel that way. Not ever."

Slowly, he turned to face Dallas. "I'll file for the rescission. More than that, I'll hire the best goddamn attorneys on this planet to make it happen. And when it's over, I'll give her away to you at the altar. I'll do all that," he said as Dallas fought his own tears, "but at the end of the day, you will still be my son. It just won't say so on a piece of paper. Deal?"

Tears welled in Dallas's eyes, and his throat was thick when he extended his hand to the man who would always be his one true dad. "Deal," he said.

And as he turned to look at his mother once more, he thought that maybe—*maybe*—he saw a hint of a smile.

34

'Til Death

Christmas Eve . . .

I wake to the feather-soft sweetness of Dallas's kisses on my cheek, my neck, the curve of my shoulder. And down, and down, and down.

When his body is between my legs and his tongue teases my belly button, I slide my fingers into his hair.

"Well, good morning," he says, peering up at me with heated eyes and an innocent grin. "Did I wake you?"

"Mmm. I was having the most wonderful dream. This incredibly sexy man was kissing my entire body. My face, my neck, my breasts. And then he went lower and lower, and his tongue was like magic. He held me down and just kept teasing and sucking until I thought I was going to burst into flames right in his arms."

"I think I'm jealous," he says. "Who was this guy?"

"Oh, just some man I'm going to marry."

"Are you? Well, in that case I have a little present for the bride."

I would answer him, but I can't because I'm gasping with pleasure from the way he's lowered his mouth to my pussy. The way he's sucking hard on my clit. He's holding my thighs wide apart, and I'm splayed out and exposed, and he's holding me so firm that I can't move or squirm or otherwise escape the assault.

I can do nothing but endure the wild pleasure of his relentless assault, and I tilt my head back, my hands fisted in the sheets as Dallas's tongue conducts a symphony on my body, his finger playing me like a fine instrument as well. It's too much—too wild, too intense—and I feel the shock of sensation building in me, starting as a low, electrical buzz in my inner thigh and then growing more and more vibrant until I lose all control over my body, and my hips are bucking and I'm crying out, calling Dallas's name and begging him to stop—then begging him to never, ever stop.

He tightens his grip on my legs and holds me in place, sucking and teasing and forcing me to ride it out until I'm so shattered that my entire body is shaking and I'm gasping for air.

"Wow," I say as I come down off a sexual high. "My last orgasm as a single woman. That was amazing."

"I'm all about the personal service." He slides up my body and kisses me as I lay back in a blissful haze.

"Wow," I repeat. "I could stay here all day."

"You better not," he says. "You're expected at a wedding in just a few hours."

I prop myself up on my elbow. "It's bad luck to see a bride on her wedding day. I think you've just doomed us."

"That's in her wedding dress. Good thing for us you're naked. But I am leaving. Dad and I are buying breakfast for the guys, then heading back here to get dressed. Mom's meeting you here in an hour, right?"

I glance at the clock, and then nod. "Stacey, too. Brody's dropping her off and then joining you."

We're in the Meadow Lane house—the house in which I spent so much of my childhood. The house that is going to be ours again as soon as Dallas and I are married. Daddy's calling it a wedding present, but Mom tells me it's really just a token. "Your father's been in a present-buying mood lately," she says. "It seems like every day he's taking me on a trip or buying me diamonds. I love it, but I really don't get it."

I do. He almost lost her. And even though she's fully recovered, he doesn't ever want to take her for granted again. And with my dad, that translates to showering her with gifts.

Dallas and I have been the recipients of his largesse as well, and though Dad hasn't said so, we both know that it's his way of apologizing. I think the fact that the Manhattan townhouse has been restored to me was apology enough, but that doesn't mean I'll turn down anything else he wants to sign over to us.

Even though we have the townhouse back, I expect we'll be living primarily in the Hamptons. After all, Deliverance is set up again in the basement.

After a long discussion with the team, Dallas decided to bring our parents into the loop, and not only is Daddy proud of what Dallas is doing, but he's perfectly content to have his son back on the Sykes payroll, knowing full well the job is mostly camouflage.

I stay in bed for another half hour after Dallas leaves, too spent to move. Then I get up and shower and put on a fluffy robe before going into the third-floor den that has been set up as a dressing room. My mom and Stacey are there, along with a girl to do my hair and makeup. It seems a bit like overkill considering we've invited less than thirty people to our wedding. But at the same time, this wedding is an event that I never dreamed would happen, and I intend to celebrate the reality of it by going into full-on princess mode.

Once I'm primped and powdered and combed and brushed to within an inch of my life, I let the women help me get dressed, a process which gives me new understanding of why women needed ladies' maids back in the day. The top of the dress is essentially a beaded corset that cinches tight at my waist and perks up my breasts. It's elegant and shows off my cleavage and shoulders.

But it's the skirt that is the showstopper. Beautifully hand embroidered with a long, removable train, the skirt sits on a wide hoop, making my waist look even smaller and giving me an overall delicate look. A princess look.

I examine myself in the mirror and know that Dallas is going to love it.

"You look beautiful," Mom says, coming up behind me. She sniffles and I hold up a hand.

"No! No crying or I'll start. And I can't. I'll smear my makeup."

"Okay," she says. "I'll cry when you're walking down the aisle."

"Deal," I say, as Stacey tells us that we need to hurry because they're ready for me.

The wedding is going to be performed in the main hall, which has been filled with flowers and temporary chairs, and we hurry to where I'm meeting my dad at the top of the stairs. We're descending together, and then proceeding down the aisle to where Dallas waits by the French doors, a stunning view of the pool behind him.

Daddy looks up as I approach, his eyes filled with such pride I almost tear up again.

"I'll tell you what I told Mom," I say. "Don't make me cry."

"No promises," he says, then kisses me on the cheek. "You look beautiful. I'm so proud of you."

We stand there alone—I didn't want attendants—and just as the first strains of music rise, my father turns to me. "You never did tell me what you want for Christmas tomorrow."

It's so absurd that I laugh.

"Trust me, Daddy," I say, "you already gave me and Dallas the best present of all."

I hear our cue, and I take my father's arm.

And then I finally walk down the stairs and my father escorts me to Dallas, then gives me away to the man I've loved my whole life. The man who was once my brother.

The man who is my best friend.

And who, in just a few minutes, will be my husband.

J. KENNER (aka Julie Kenner) is the *New York Times, USA Today, Publishers Weekly, Wall Street Journal,* and #1 international bestselling author of over seventy novels, novellas, and short stories.

Though known primarily for her award-winning and international best-selling erotic romances (including the Stark, Stark International, Dirtiest, and Most Wanted series) that have reached as high as #2 on the *New York Times* bestseller list, Kenner has been writing full-time for over a decade in a variety of genres, including paranormal and contemporary romance, "chicklit" suspense, urban fantasy, and paranormal mommy lit.

Kenner has been praised by *Publishers Weekly* as an author with a "flair for dialogue and eccentric characterizations" and by *RT Book Reviews* for having "cornered the market on sinfully attractive, dominant antiheroes and the women who swoon for them." A four-time finalist for Romance Writers of America's prestigious RITA award, Kenner took home the first RITA trophy awarded in the category of erotic romance in 2014 for her novel *Claim Me* (book 2 of her Stark Trilogy).

Her books have sold well over a million copies and are published in over twenty countries.

jkenner.com

Facebook.com/jkennerbooks

@juliekenner